Bring Me More Stories: Tales of the Sephardim

t

By
Sally Benforado

Floricanto Press

Floricanto Press
650 Castro Street, Suite 120-331
Mountain View, California 94041-2055
www.floricantopress.com

Bring Me More Stories

About the Author

SALLY BENFORADO was born in Syracuse, NY, and has lived in Buffalo, NY, Boston, MA, and England, as well as in Madison, WI, where she has resided for the past 38 years. She teaches creative writing in a community-founded program for students ranging in age from 60 to 99 years. She and her late husband Joe had six children, and have six grandchildren.

Her short stories, articles and poems have appeared in numerous national and international publications including *The Christian Science Monitor*, *Woman's Day*, *Lady's Circle*, *The Villager*, *Wisconsin State Journal*, Capital Times, St. Croix Review, Appleton Post Crescent, *North American Mentor*, *Port Cities*, *Madison Magazine*, *The Feminist Connection*, *Revista/Review Interamericana*, *The Snowy Egret*, and *The New Southern Literary Review*

PREFACE

I have taught writing classes for a number of years, working with people of all ages; and although I enjoy working in fiction and other forms, my favorite medium has always been the writing down of family stories. History, if you will. I feel these tales are important to record. They will always remain less than a complete story, being more like the broken bits of pottery or fragmentary pieces of a puzzle. They represent a colorful facet of the population influx into the United States early in this century, reminding us of the millions who came from all over the globe and stayed to make this new land their home.

We need to know who our ancestors were, what they experienced, and how they lived. How can we know who we are unless we know where we came from?

The stories in this book are about descendants of Jews who were exiled from Spain in 1942 during the Inquisition. These *Sephardim*, as they are called, wandered the Mediterranean seaboard, settling ultimately in such countries as Italy, France, Greece, Turkey and Yugoslavia, where they clustered in tight communities, maintaining their language, liturgy, and customs. Always these Sephardim dreamed of returning one day to their homes in Spain or Portugal. Many of the families at one time possessed house keys, large and ancient, which were said to be keys to the homes from which their ancestors had fled in the late 15th century. Then, in the early 1900's many Sephardim braved crossing the Atlantic Ocean and came to live in the United States.

Since I come from a family whose Irish/English roots in

America are deep, I sometimes view my first generation American Sephardic husband and his family as exotics. I have had a longtime fascination with their differences. It is, in fact, probably one of the reasons I married him. At the same time, as a writer, I can separate myself from an awe of their colorful splendor and write of them with a certain detachment.

When the first edition of this book was published in December 1986, I gave my mother-in-law, Mathilde, who had told me many of the stories, a copy. She was at that time living in the Sephardic Home in Queens, New York, and she was so pleased to have the book that she carried it everywhere she went, and she showed it to anyone who showed the slightest interest. Eventually the book became so tattered that I presented her with a fresh copy!

Relatives and friends also showed interest and sometimes mentioned that they had a Sephardic story that would interest me. After they told me their story, I would applaud and suggest that they get a notebook and write the story. They always laughed and said, "Oh, we don't need to write the stories down; we all know the stories by heart." And that was true. However, time moves on, generations change, and those who knew those stories so well are no longer with us. In the years since *Bring Me A Story* was first published, both my mother-in-law and my father-in-law have passed on, and so has my beloved husband Joe.

So I can no longer ask them to tell me stories. But I have gotten a number of those stories down on paper. Mathilde was my best and most willing storyteller. And I did once persuade Mark, my father-in-law, to tell me a story. Then, a few years before his death, my Joe wrote down a few stories, two of which appear in the new edition. I'm so glad that he got those stories on paper!

So, after you have read these stories of mine, you might want to grab a cup of coffee and a notebook and start writing down some of your family stories. If you can't think of any, why not call one of your aunties or uncles and invite them to tell you a story?

ENJOY!

Sally Benforado
Madison, Wisconsin

*I dedicate this small book
to a gifted storyteller,
my late mother-in-law Mathilde Benforado,
whose love has warmed me
for almost six decades*

Table of Contents

Prologue:
Bring Me a Story

Let me tell you about Moïse, my mother-in-law's brother, and how he came to America. When he was already a jaunty fellow of 17, she was far down the line of a long procession of sisters and was quite small. Mathilde doesn't remember much about him then, and only got to know Moïse well much later, when she lived with him and his wife in New York City.

My mother-in-law, Mathilde, is a splendid teller of tales that are crammed always with vivid descriptions and pithy quotes from conversations long remembered. If I have the good luck to be present when she is in a storytelling mood, all I have to do is switch on my mental tape recorder. If I listen hard enough, I can, even years later, get down the story intact, remembering almost perfectly her tone of voice, her turn of phrase, even the way she tilts her head and purses her lips as she tries to put into words the essence of the situation.

However, this one time I was out of luck. My husband, Joe, was to visit his parents, who live now in Florida, and I was to remain at home with the children. "Bring me a story," I begged him. "Bring me back a tale, one of Mom's."

This he did—he brought back the story of Moïse's coming to America in the closing years of the 19th century. It was interesting, undeniably so, but somehow curiously flat in the telling. In my elliptical, chauvinistic way, I blamed the bearer of the tale. He hadn't listened. I mumbled to myself, as I tried in vain to get Moïse's adventure down on paper. It's his fault; he doesn't know how to capture his own mother's flavor, her charming way of recreating the past. And the story was not written.

On another visit I went along too, and when Mom and I

were sitting in the kitchen together I said, "Tell me about Moïse, how he came to America." And she laughed and tilted her head and told me the same story with the same curious flatness. What was happening? I couldn't understand it. Was she losing her touch? Where would my stories come from now?

I brooded about it at length, and finally I understood. Of course, the story had to be told by her in that flat fashion. She didn't see it happen. She was too young. It's just a story she was herself told. Aha! So be it. It's still worth the telling to you, because it will probably lead to another story.

Moïse and his older brother, Eli, along with his parents and his many sisters, aunts, uncles and cousins, all lived in a community of Sephardic Jews near Smyrna, Turkey, in the late years of the 19th century. Centuries ago during the Spanish Inquisition, their ancestors had fled from Spain and journeyed in search of a home. Some Sephardim settled in the south of France, some in Italy, in Greece, in Turkey, and in spots all the way around the Mediterranean basin. Once settled in Turkey, these Sephardim had remained there for a very long time, clustered in a tight community where they continued to speak Spanish, which over the course of time became increasingly archaic.

There must, however, have been present even in this tight community the same restiveness that permeated southern European countries at that time. Did all the young people truly believe that in America the streets were paved with gold? Who knows? What were they all in search of, as they climbed aboard all the ships and sailed westward?

Moïse, too, must have had his dreams, his hopes. He's long dead and we can't ask, but perhaps he dreamed, even as a schoolboy in Turkey, of coming to the glorious new world and making his fortune. Our story begins with the one night when he didn't return home. His parents didn't worry excessively; they assumed he had spent the night with friends or relatives in Smyrna, where he attended school. However, the next day his father, Papa David, went into the city and asked about his son. No one had seen him at school; no one had seen him anywhere. Eventually Papa David went down to the pier where the steamers from Europe came in.

"Have you seen my son?" he asked again and again.

"Oh, but yes," someone said at last. "I saw Moïse yesterday, boarding the steamer for Marseille."

And here is where one gets the flatness, the missing emotion. Mathilde, my mother-in-law, does not speak of her father's sadness. She is more apt to dwell intently upon what her brother had been wearing. "A white linen suit, very handsome, well cut in the latest style. And a panama hat." Mathilde loves clothes, fashions, fine materials; and here, as this beautiful image takes shape in my greedy imagination, I think that perhaps the tiny Mathilde might be reaching far back in her memory to the vision of her handsome brother wearing this magnificent costume.

When next the family got news of the wandering one, it was in the form of a letter from Marseille. "I don't wish to remain here," Moïse wrote. There are limited opportunities. Will you perhaps send me sufficient money that I may go to New York to join my brother, Eli?"

This the father did, and perhaps both Papa and his wife, Joya, were happy to think that their sons would be together in the New World, and that some sort of family life would be ongoing there. I can't help but be sad though, even 80 years later, for Joya. Surely she, the mother, wept bitter tears.

The journey to America by ship was a hard one. The weather was incredibly bad, with high winds and severe storms. Moïse was robbed, losing his identity cards as well as his money. He was in steerage, and over the course of the weeks of passage, he was sick and couldn't eat. He grew thinner and thinner.

At long last the ship arrived in New York harbor, and all the immigrants were shunted off onto Ellis Island. The officials demanded then to know who would speak for Moïse in America, "Why, my brother, Eli," said the poor fellow. And Eli was sent for.

But when Eli came, having been summoned away from the cigarette factory where he worked, he didn't recognize his brother. Who was this drab scarecrow of a fellow wearing a filthy suit that hung upon his scrawny frame? His beautiful white linen suit had long lost its crispness and by this time it was limp and gray.

"I refuse to acknowledge this person," Eli cried immediately, whereupon Moïse fell upon him.

"Oh Eli, my brother! Surely you know me?"

Eli backed away, fastidiously brushing at his clothing, and shot off a bombardment of questions. "Who are you, anyway? Your parents, what are their names? Where did you come from, where did you go to school?"

All these questions and more, Moïse answered perfectly, but only when Eli demanded to know "Your sisters, tell me their names," and Moïse rattled them off without hesitation, from Cadem who was the oldest on down to Mary, who was the youngest, only then did Eli come closer. And, getting past the grime on his brother's face, the quivering lips, and the hollows in his cheeks, only then did he look deep into his despairing eyes, and only then did he shout joyously, "It *is* you, Moïse! Welcome! I am so happy you have come to join me in America."

Old World/New World
Turkish Fairy Tale

At the turn of the century, families everywhere tended to be large, and Papa David's family was no exception. Very much the family man, he sat contentedly one evening in the center of his large cluster of daughters, his wife, plus a sprinkling of other relatives who were living with them. The traditional red fez worn by all Turkish men, even the Sephardim, hung low on his forehead and his eyes twinkled. Papa David was happy to be at home. He filled his pipe and graciously permitted one of his daughters to light it.

"Thank you, my dear," he said. "Let me see, what is your name?" And he roared with laughter, for it was a pet joke with him that he had so many daughters that he could not possibly remember their names.

"I have a surprise," said Papa, patting his pocket.

"A letter, a letter!" cried young Mathilde, climbing into his lap and looking up at him with her large gray eyes.

"From Ezra," said Papa, "that young man from America who has seen a photograph of Cadem and wants to marry her."

"Is that his photograph, Papa?" asked one of the girls, seeing that he was holding something else.

"Yes," he said, surrendering it to one of the many outstretched hands. Cries of "Oh!" "Handsome!" "What a nice moustache!" filled the room. Papa rattled the letter feeling that he was not getting enough attention.

"Ezra feels," said Papa, "it is only fair that Cadem should see a picture of him before he comes to visit us."

"When is he coming, Papa?" asked Cadem, sitting very still. Only when she spoke did the others turn to look at her, this beautiful young woman with the fair complexion, dark, wavy hair piled on top of her head, and wide, gray eyes similar to Mathilde's.

"Tomorrow," said Papa nonchalantly, then shook with laughter at the pandemonium let loose.

"What!"

"Tomorrow?"

"Impossible!"

"All the way from America?"

"The letter," said Papa, "is postmarked from France. He was planning to take the small boat from there and arrive today. We go to meet the boat tomorrow."

"Who's going, Papa?"

"Me!"

"Me!"

"No, me!"

"Mama spoke. "Only Cadem, Papa and myself. It will be hard enough on the young man, just meeting us, and it would be impossible with seven more girls."

Suddenly Cadem, who had been sitting so quietly, burst into tears. Papa looked concerned. Pulling out a large handkerchief, he pressed it onto Cadem's hand and patted her upon the head.

"Don't cry," he said. "You don't have to marry him if you don't want to."

"But I do," sobbed Cadem. "I want to live in America. But how do I know I will like him? And how can I leave my family?"

Mama kissed Cadem, saying to her, "Don't you think about this foolishness any more tonight. It's time all you girls went to bed anyway." She smiled at Cadem until Cadem smiled back, then all the girls tumbled out of the room and went upstairs. Along the way, little Mathilde seized a fold of Cadem's long skirt, looked up at her and said, "Dear Sister, if you marry and go to America, I will come to be with you." And Cadem squeezed her young sister's hand tightly.

The parents sat quietly, Papa puffing on his pipe, until Mama heaved a big sigh.

"Mama," said Papa, "do you want Cadem to marry this young man?"

"Do you?"

"Well," he hedged, "would you like her to marry him, I mean if she wanted to?"

"I . . . don't know," said Mama. "He comes from a good family. But America still seems so far away, even though two of our sons have gone there to seek their fortunes."

"I know," Papa sighed. "They do say the opportunities for young people are very great there, although I for one do not truly believe the streets are paved with gold."

Then he added, "If you don't want her to marry him, she won't. I can take care of everything."

"You mustn't interfere."

"Me? Interfere?" Papa looked hurt. "Well, let us not think about it any more tonight." And he put a comforting arm about Mama, and they sat quietly together.

The next afternoon Cadem, Mama and Papa were on their way into Smyrna to meet the steamer. For a time no one said anything, there was only the clop-clopping of the horse, then Papa broke the silence.

"We are going to no one's funeral."

No one responded to his joke, and there was silence again until Mama made conversation.

"David, did you finish your business in town this morning?"

"Business?" he asked absently.

"The business you said you had to do in town."

"What?—er—oh! Yes," said Papa, putting a hand up to his moustache.

Once again, the only sound was the beating of the horse's hooves on the road. Cadem sat quietly between her parents. She was dressed in her finest dress and wearing a large hat.

"Look," said Mama suddenly. "The Bensousanes are coming out of their place in their carriage. I wonder where they are going."

Papa looked straight ahead at his horse. Cadem turned about to wave at Luna Bensousane, who was eighteen like herself, but blonde, not dark like Cadem. The Bensousane carriage was pulling alongside of theirs.

"We'll meet you at the boat," called out Mr. Bensousane. And then their carriage pulled ahead and went rolling on down the sunny road.

Mama, Papa and Cadem all stared straight ahead, saying nothing, until they arrived at the place where the boat was to dock. Then Papa jumped out and helped the women down. Cadem saw Luna talking with some of their friends and ran over to visit with them.

"David," said Mama. "What was the business you had to attend to this morning?"

He pulled at his moustache. "Oh . . ." he started.

"Wait," she said, holding up her hand. "Don't tell me, I know. You went to the Bensousanes'. But why?"

"I thought it might be a good idea to give Ezra a choice of more than one girl."

Mama stared silently at Papa, who yanked nervously at his moustache.

"I did wrong?" he asked. "I was only trying to help."

"David, you know we have eight daughters to marry off. If you had wanted to show Ezra other girls, you could have first shown him one of our own daughters. Must you marry off all the girls in the neighborhood and leave our girls to be old maids? This young man from America is rich. He would be a good catch for our daughter."

He shrugged. Women were hard to understand. He had expected Mama to be pleased at his maneuvers.

"We had better join the others," he said meekly. "The boat is docking."

"We need not worry," Mama said. Our daughter is much prettier than the Bensousane child." And she put her arm through his and they walked over to where the others waited.

"You are just in time," cried Mr. Bensousane to Papa. "They are already coming off the boat."

"Hello, Rae. Hello, Moussa," said Papa, greeting the old friends, then pulled Ezra's photograph out of his pocket, while the two mothers smiled at each other politely, but distantly.

"There he is," said Papa. And he pointed to a tall young man standing where the yellow sand met the water.

They went forward and Cadem and Luna joined their parents, the two girls with their arms about each other.

Their respective mothers beckoned to them and each was carefully inspected before being pressed forth to meet the young man.

Photo still in hand, Papa said, "I am Cadem's father, and you are . . ."

"I am Ezra," said the man, extending his hand, and smiling at Papa, then quickly looking about for Cadem. His eyes popped when he saw before him not one but two sets of parents, and not one but two young girls, one dark and the other blond, both very pretty. Papa performed introductions, and everyone began laughing and talking and someone suggested going to an outdoor café.

"Wonderful," said Papa. "Just the thing. Here, Moussa, you take Ezra along with you, and we'll meet at the café."

Mama, Papa and Cadem were again edged together in the carriage. For a time no one said anything. Papa kept busy with his driving, uncomfortable from knowing that his wife was giving him cold stares over their daughter's head. Cadem broke the silence.

"He's very handsome, isn't he," she said.

Both parents straightened to look at Cadem. Her face was flushed and her eyes were starry.

"Yes, dear," said her mother, tightening up her lips and throwing significant glances at Papa.

"Well, we're here," announced Papa, thinking that he would never understand women. Competition could always seem to change their minds about things. He jumped out and fastened his horse to a post, then turned to help the women down but saw that Ezra had already gotten out of the Bensousane carriage and was helping them. Mama was talking and laughing and Cadem was just gazing at him.

Mama came over close to Papa. "Now, see what you have done?" she hissed in his ear. "Brought another girl along so Ezra could choose, and Cadem is in love with him."

"Love, perhaps," said Papa. "But we don't yet know if she

wants to marry him."

"Yes, we do," said Mama. "She told me just now. Why not? He's rich and handsome. And we have so many daughters."

Papa fingered his moustache. "I have made a mistake," he said sadly.

His wife smiled. "Never mind," she said, having scored her point. "Just leave everything to me." And taking his arm, she led him over to the others.

Moussa and his wife and Luna were already seated at a table. They started moving over to make room for everyone.

"There is no room," said Mama. "Why don't we sit at the next table? Ezra, perhaps you would like to sit between Cadem and myself?" And she threw a triumphant glance at Mrs. Bensousane. Ezra sat down.

"Tell us about America," Mama demanded.

Ezra smiled nervously. "Oh, a wonderful country." Then he stopped and glanced over at the next table where Luna sat with her parents.

Mama frowned, "And New York," she said. "Are the buildings as high as they say?"

"Oh, very tall," said Ezra. "You get a crick in your neck from looking at them." He paused. "Excuse me," he said politely, then walked over to the next table and stood talking with the Bensousane family.

Papa turned to Cadem whose face under the shade of her wide hat was wistful.

"Mama," said Cadem, "do you think he likes Luna better?"

"Of course not."

"But her hair is so blond and beautiful."

"Yes, but she has freckles." Mama patted her daughter's arm. "Drink your tea and leave everything to Papa and me."

Ezra was returning to the table.

"New York sounds very nice," said Mama to him. "But it must be lonely."

"Lonely?" said the puzzled young man.

"Yes," asked Mama. "Being there all alone, without a family, I mean."

"Yes, of course," said Ezra. "Oh—er—what wonderful tea."

And he all but buried his nose in the cup.

Mama frowned and was quiet while everyone drank the tea. As they were making ready to leave, Mama kicked Papa under the table. "Get him alone," she whispered, "and ask him."

"Ask him?"

"Yes."

Papa thought hard, then drawing a breath said to Ezra, "I'd like to show you my horse, a fine animal." And Mama, Papa and Ezra walked over to the horse, while Cadem climbed up into the carriage.

"Tell me," said Papa softly, stroking the horse, "which one do you like?"

"Which . . . horse?" said Ezra confused.

"No, no," said Papa, "which girl?"

Ezra jumped; the horse, startled, rose up on its hind legs; and as the women screamed, the horse began trotting down the street; but Cadem wasn't alone in the carriage, for Ezra had jumped in and was beside her pulling hard on the reins trying to make the horse stop.

Automatically, Papa put an arm about his wife as they stood looking after the disappearing carriage.

"No," Mama called out suddenly. "No, Moussa, do not follow them. Ezra will bring the carriage back." So Moussa climbed down, and his wife was able to stop pleading with him not to go.

Everyone stood waiting, not saying anything, and after a while the horse, quiet now, reappeared with a radiant and rosy couple in the carriage behind him. Ezra helped Cadem down, and she was immediately clasped in her mother's arms to be cried over. However, Mama also managed to signal to Papa that he should ask Ezra the question.

"Thank you for saving my daughter," said Papa to Ezra, who said nothing. "Now as we were saying," and he held on tightly to the horse this time, "which girl do you prefer?"

"Cadem, of course."

"Not Luna?"

"She is very pretty, but she is blond, not dark and beautiful like Cadem. I have wanted to marry Cadem ever since I saw her photograph."

"But," said Papa, "you spent so much time talking with Luna."

"I was just asking if she thought Cadem would marry me. It is *your* daughter I wish to marry, sir, . . . with your permission, of course."

"I will be proud to have you for a son," said Papa, "if my daughter wishes to marry you."

"I think she will not mind," said Ezra.

"Let us tell Mama."

"But oughtn't I ask Cadem first?"

"Oh yes, I had forgotten how these things are done. Yes, that is the thing to do," said Papa. "But first I must tell Moussa that you have decided to marry Cadem, so he and his wife will know you are no longer eligible for Luna."

"Moussa," he called. "Come here. I think my horse has a sore foot."

Moussa came over and all three men looked at the foot, while Papa said, "He wants to marry Cadem. Is it all right with you, Moussa?"

"Yes, my wife may be a little angry. But then, she probably would have been angry if things had worked out the other way and Ezra had married Luna."

"Moussa went to his wife and whispered to her and Luna. The wife frowned but Luna smiled.

Papa spoke to the waiter, who returned with a jug and some glasses. "A toast to the future bride and groom," he announced.

Mama looked at him. "I should think you would give Ezra an opportunity to propose to Cadem without your shouting it from the housetops first."

"Oh, I am sorry, Ezra. I forgot," said Papa. "Forgive me Cadem. I was only trying to help."

Ezra smiled, saying, "You did. I probably couldn't have said it myself." Then he turned to Cadem.

"Will you?" he asked softly.

"Yes," she said, whereupon Luna ran over to kiss Cadem and Ezra, Mama and Mrs. Bensousane burst into tears and threw their arms about each other, each to comfort the other, and the horse rose up on its hind legs again. Papa and Moussa quieted the animal. After a while the women stopped crying. Then the waiter poured, and as everyone sipped they shouted wonderful things to each other, and everyone seemed full of joy.

Later, when Papa and Mama were riding in the carriage down the road leading home, Mama said, "That was a clever thing you did this afternoon."

And he replied modestly, as if he had planned all along to make the horse jump so Ezra could leap into the runaway carriage and rescue Cadem, "Oh, it was nothing."

Then he put his arm about his wife, who seemed to be feeling cold, and he whistled into the gathering dusk what should have been a merry tune.

The Procession

Like the wind the child is running, her short sturdy legs turning and churning. She is on her way home from school. She is seven years old, in the very early 1900's, in Izmir, Turkey. Her long curls are flying; her dark pinafore is buttoned over her school costume, as she approaches home.

She whirls through the open and welcoming gates, skims across the quiet courtyard, and races towards the dark cavernous kitchen. Mathilde is so hungry — it's been a long day at the Convent school. But she also needs to ask her mother something. And she doesn't want anyone else to hear.

Privacy can be a problem in this large household. Mathilde's spirits droop as she enters the kitchen, to see her sisters all working together with Mama at the large table. However, she patiently joins them. She will just have to wait, that is all.

"Ah, *mi alma*," says her mother fondly. And Mathilde, taking for granted this adulation, accepts the snack Mama offers - a handful of nuts and raisins. She stands; her feet firmly planted on the old stone floor of the kitchen, nibbling the nuts and the raisins slowly, one at a time. She is still eager to talk with her mother privately, but she can't help but be captivated any time she has a chance to work alongside of her big sisters.

She studies her mother and sisters as they continue with their work. She regards them with awe; they seem so grown up, so serious, with their grave faces, their sense of importance in the work they are doing.

How quick and nimble their fingers are. They are making biscotchos, taking bits of dough from a large bowl and rolling them into finger shapes, which they form into circles. Then they carefully sprinkle sesame seeds over the tops. Smiling, her mother Joya hands her a piece of dough, and Mathilde solemnly begins the process of rolling the fat wad of dough into a thin strip, carefully forming it into a circle. Joya hovers, then hands her a tiny handful of sesame seeds, which Mathilde sprinkles over the top.

Biding her time, Mathilde hums contentedly. For her, coming home is the best part of the day. Although she loves school and is a favorite with the nuns, who always applaud her efforts at handwriting and praise her needlework effusively, she really relishes coming home to the serene household, her mother, and her many sisters.

You might well ask what a little Sephardic Jewish girl was doing attending a convent school. Simple enough. Mathilde's father wanted his daughters to get an education; this, he felt, would help them to obtain husbands. Hence he had enrolled Mathilde in the convent.

Most of the other children at school were Turkish or Greek, and Catholic. Did Mathilde know she was different? Did her classmates know that she and her family spoke Ladino, an archaic form of Spanish? Did they understand that her ancestors had left Spain hundreds of years ago because of the threat of the Inquisition? Somehow it didn't seem to matter. Mathilde always felt accepted and loved wherever she went.

In fact, this very day Mathilde had been singled out for attention by one of the nuns. She was bursting with excitement, wanting to tell her mother what the nun had suggested and to plead with her mother to allow her to do it. Still she stood there, watching her sisters and waiting.

The biscotchos were ready for the oven, and Mathilde's sisters drifted off to another part of the large kitchen to do the cleaning up. Here was the opportunity Mathilde had been waiting for. Cheeks aflame with excitement, Mathilde sidled closer. "Mama," she said, turning to Joya, who stood, leaning against the long table.

Joya leaned towards this little daughter, this gift, and stroked her hair. "Yes, *mi alma*," she murmured. She knew that Mathilde was about to ask something of her, and whatever it was, she would probably say yes. Joya could refuse this one nothing. Mathilde had been a gift, a *mazeltov*, born to her parents after the tragic loss of a boy child, one of twins, who died in the first summer of his life. Joya, who had already borne several children, found herself ill after the birth of twins, a boy and a girl. Unable to nurse both, she handed the female infant over to a wet nurse and, of course, kept the all important boy child with her. Although unwell and completely lacking energy, Joya did the best she could with the tiny boy child, nursing him to the best of her ability. Under the care of the wet nurse, the little girl child grew plump and strong and eventually came home to live with her family again. But the boy child did not fare so well.

Perhaps Joya's milk supply was inadequate, perhaps Joya was too ill and run down to feed him enough. At any rate, he sickened and died, and there was great sadness in the family. Mixed in with the grief there was also a subtle fear, a sort of threat that this large thriving family had somehow lost its luck. This sense of sorrow and doom, although not overwhelming, did touch upon all the family, the children as well as the adults.

When Joya again became pregnant a year or two after the baby boy's death and bore eventually a girl child, both Joya and David felt blessed and happy again. They thought of naming her "*Mazeltov*", but they already had living with them a young niece with that name. And so they called their newest child Mathilde instead – but always they thought of her as a bit of rare good fortune, a *mazeltov*, and they loved her with a very special love.

"Mama," she said again, and her mother again smiled and said "Yes, *mi alma*."

Mathilde leaned towards her mother, cupped a small hand about her mother's ear and whispered something. Joya drew back, just slightly, and stared. Joya's brow was furrowed with tiny lines and she seemed puzzled, almost incredulous. "*Kualo?*" she said in astonishment. Her eyes grew large.

Mathilde leaned towards her once more, wrapped a small arm about her mother's neck, and whispered some more. Her sisters continued to work, but glanced at their mother and little sister from time to time as Mathilde gestured and made waving motions with her fingers. "And Mama," she said softly. "I won't, after all, be inside the church itself."

Joya sat back and was silent, her mouth shaped like an O, as she studied this small child, this *mazeltov*. Mathilde held her breath.

Finally her mother spoke. "Ah, well," she said, sighing heavily. "How can it do any harm? And, I suppose it could be considered a part of your schoolwork? Your father wants you to do well in school, Mathilde." She paused, and then spoke again. "Yes, you may do what the nuns have asked of you."

Mathilde clapped her hands for joy. Her eyes sparkled. "Truly, Mama?" she asked.

And her Mother nodded. "Yes, truly," she said.

Mathilde drew in a breath and prepared to gallop from the cavernous kitchen. Joya held her by the wrist.

"One thing," said Joya softly, "and this I think you understand. Your father is not to know."

And Mathilde, understanding, shook her head from side to side, lips clenched together tightly. They both returned to their work, preparing the biscotchos. Soon Papa David came home.

"Joya," he said impatiently. "Why are you all still working in the kitchen? When will dinner be ready at this rate?" And Mathilde noted that her mother didn't tell him how hard they'd all been working, but instead jollied him into sitting down on the sofa and reading the newspaper.

Soon the biscotchos were in the oven, and her sisters swiftly cleaned up the kitchen, and before too long the table was set and dinner was ready. As was the custom, each of the daughters came up to Papa David, knelt down and bent over to kiss the ring on his finger. Every evening they did this as a gesture of respect. Then he and Mama sat at table, joined by the daughters, and the meal was served. As always, Mama sighed just as they were about to begin eating, and said, "Let us remember our sons in America. May they be well." And Papa sighed and said, "I miss my boys. Sometimes I hate being the only man in the house." And then he laughed. And finally, they began eating.

Mathilde thought about what Papa had just said. She felt

sad for him. She too missed Eli and Moïse. However, it had never occurred to her before that Papa missed them too. She thought about that for a long time before she went to sleep that night. Papa must feel very lonely at times, she thought, and she tried to imagine what their household would be like if there were swarms of men and boys around and, perhaps, only one woman.

And so it came to pass that on a school day morning a few days later, on a Feast Day when David, Mathilde's father, was walking near the cathedral square on his way to a business meeting, he spotted a procession of young people, following the priests, the crucifixes and other paraphernalia, and a statue of the Virgin Mary. The procession was wending its way about the square. The day was warm, with the sun golden like the crucifix and the sky was blue to match the painted flowing garments of Mary the Virgin.

David always enjoyed a processional scene, and he paused to take in the ceremonial march, along with the other passers by. Although this religion was not his, and the customs were unfamiliar to him, there were certain obvious similarities, and he smiled. How different can a rabbi be from a priest, he thought, and we all have certain relics we hold dear, the torah is what we would carry in a processional, and children — well, children, they are the same, everywhere, and they all love parades.

The processional was drawing near now and he stepped back slightly, to give them room. Past him and all the other onlookers came the priests and their acolytes, with their incense burners, the large cross, and finally the handsome statue of Mary, followed by a flock of children. A few of the children had apparently been chosen to hold long ribbons that extended from the statue. David smiled. Charming, he thought.

Then, as the flock moved on, and proceeded along another side of the square, David blinked. He stared. That little girl in the dark pinafore, the one with the flowing hair that curled, the one who held lavender ribbon proudly — it looked so much like — he could swear it must have been— he closed his eyes.

After a moment, he reopened his eyes. Again he looked at the processional, now on the far side of the square from him. He could see that little girl. No, it wasn't Mathilde. Definitely it wasn't Mathilde. That would be impossible. He walked on quickly.

Tocado

(Ladino for headdress, head covering, elaborate hairdo)

Joya hadn't even noticed him at first. He looked so much like other men who were bustling about importantly in the train station. She smiled. In appearance David was becoming daily more like a European - a Frenchman or an Italian. That suit he was wearing, so different from what he would have worn a few years earlier.

She sat, in her usual fashion, legs triangled outward, hands resting loosely on heavy thighs. Her head was held high and her gray eyes were alert as she gazed at the passing scene. Life in Turkey these days was changing rapidly, as the businessmen and politicians came increasingly under the influence of the western countries. As her husband David approached her, they greeted one another with the formality expected of a married couple meeting in public, bowing and nodding before moving slowly towards the waiting train. Joya had just spent a rare day in town visiting with her sisters, and she basked still in the relaxed aura of the pleasant day. She walked proudly, aware that her costume reflected a certain financial and cultural standing. Her jacket was a handsome brocaded one, lined with fur. Like many Sephardic women in the early 1900's she wore this jacket instead of the more fashionable full-length coat that most European women would have worn. And instead of covering shorn hair with a wig, as Ashkenazi Jewish women would have done, Joya was *tocada*, which meant that she had covered her luxuriant dark hair with a black velvet turban embellished center front with a large jeweled pin, a third eye so to speak.

They stepped into a second-class compartment, which was only partially filled. Joya placed her parcels on an overhead rack and then sat down. She made herself small, indicating smilingly to her husband that she was preparing a special space for him. However, instead of seating himself, David stood silently before her. He cleared his throat. She looked up inquiringly.

"Joya, I am joining my acquaintances in the first class seats." He held up his ticket as evidence.

Joya's mouth dropped open in surprise. "But David," she said, "we always sit together when we travel by train."

"Yes, but - well," he said.

Joya stood abruptly and reached up to retrieve her parcels. David interrupted her with a touch of his hand.

"No, my wife," he said.

"Such nonsense," she said in quiet anger. "Simply purchase a first class ticket for me, and I will join you and your acquaintances. When did you begin to travel first class by the way?"

He was vague. "Oh - somewhat recently. My European colleagues tend to go first class and - well, after all, business is business." He became aware that the compartments were filling up. "I must go or I will lose my place." He leaned over and patted her hand. "The trip is not a long one," he murmured comfortingly. "We will proceed together homeward from the train." He left.

Joya stared at the well tailored back of the husband who had suddenly become a stranger. Her brow, which was generally serene and smooth, was furrowed. Her relaxed body had become tense and her hands were clenched. The train was moving.

Joya's fellow passengers were eyeing her curiously. Obviously they were fascinated by the little interchange between her husband and herself. Joya felt humiliated. She shrank into her seat, attempting to make herself even smaller, perhaps invisible.

She stared at her fists. With an effort she flattened them out, palms down, then turned them over for observation. They were work-worn surely, but how else could they be expected to look? All those children, and all that cooking and cleaning and sewing to be done. With an effort she attempted to bring her

knees together - she still felt she was taking up too much space
- but it was difficult. She sighed.

Up to now, she had been well satisfied with her busy
productive life: their large family at home, including even at
times aged aunts or maiden cousins, with nowhere else to live;
her cooking and baking; overseeing the seamstress who came
in periodically to make clothing for everyone. And even though
the older daughters were now able to help in the kitchen, and
the eldest one was now entrusted with the important task of
transporting the breads and other such items to the town bakery,
there was still so much to do. Yet, she'd always considered
herself fortunate, a partner in the marriage, an alliance of two
equals. Joya sighed again. She could feel a headache creeping
in through her left temple.

The train was already coming into Bournebad, their station.
Joya rose with dignity, gathered up her parcels, and waited.
Aware that she might be watched, she stepped from the
compartment with head held high. David was already on the
platform, ready to greet her, although he turned back carelessly
to exchange a few words with his new colleagues.

Ordinarily Joya would have waited for David to signal that
he was ready to begin the journey to their home, but this turning
away from her was simply the last straw. She took off, leaving
him to follow her. She was moving along so rapidly that she
astonished herself. She fairly charged up the long hill that led
to their pink stucco house.

She pressed the bell at their outer gate, and soon their oldest
daughter Cadem appeared, glancing at her mother in surprise.
"Where is Father?" she asked.

Joya scorned to reply, merely jerking her head in the direction
of town to indicate that he was coming.

Cadem shrugged and moved aside to let her mother through
the open gate into the peace of their inner courtyard. Wisely,
Cadem prepared Turkish coffee and soon had Joya settled
comfortably with a tiny cup of the sweet hot liquid in her hand.
"Mama, tell me what has happened," she said, and Joya poured
out the story of her humiliating experience, in a voice that
quivered with anger. "And so," she said, winding down finally,

"I was so angry with him that I refused to even accompany him home."

Cadem surveyed her mother thoughtfully. "Mama, you know what the trouble is?"

Joya bristled. "Trouble? What do you mean, trouble? All I know is I was insulted and humiliated."

"Mama," said Cadem patiently. "Your trouble is - you are too old-fashioned." Cadem paused to pat her beautifully coiffed head, before continuing. "The world is changing so rapidly. Even Turkey is changing. You are not keeping up with the times. Papa is."

"What's this - to keep up with the times?" said Joya impatiently. "I dress well, I always look nice. Don't I?"

Cadem disappeared for a moment and returned with an oval hand mirror. "Here," she said to her mother. "Look at yourself."

Joya studied herself. "And - so?" she said finally.

"So," said Cadem. "You cover your beautiful hair with that old-time cloth thing. You wear a dumpy jacket instead of a new long coat from Paris..."

Joya interrupted her. "I wear the clothes of a traditional Sephardic woman," she said proudly. "Like my mother before me."

"Yes," said Cadem. "And your husband is ashamed of you. He refused to ride in the same train carriage with you. He prefers to sit among the fashionable Europeans."

Joya threw up her hands in despair. "But what can I do?"

Cadem was ready. "Here's what you can do." She lifted the headgear from her mother's head. She touched her mother's thick glossy hair lovingly. "Look, it's all flattened down from wearing that thing," she said scornfully. "Let me fix it."

And she drew a comb and small brush from her pocket and began to coax Joya's hair into natural springing curls and waves. As Joya watched in the mirror, her eyes began to sparkle and her mouth curved into a smile.

Cadem worked steadily. "And when we're finished with your hair, we'll talk about a new coat from Paris," she said.

Joya opened her mouth to protest, but said nothing. She continued to stare at her changing image with absorbed fascination.

Joya's transformation was completed just as David arrived, accompanied by young Mathilde. He'd met their little daughter on her way home from school. "Oh, Mama, you look so beautiful," cried the child, interrupting Cadem and her mother Joya who were laughing together. Cadem stood by Joya who sat proudly, her fists again on her thighs, her head held high, and her mouth spread wide with laughter. Upon a small table beside her were newspapers and magazines with pictures of the latest fashions in coats.

Cadem eyed her father. "Papa," she said. "Men aren't the only creatures capable of change. We women can change too." Cadem yanked the *tocado* headdress from the lap of her mother and flung it to the stone floor. "Mama, you needn't ever travel second class again."

David's hands straightened on little Mathilde's shoulders, as he held her in front of him. He looked from his wife to his daughter, then to the abandoned headgear, whose jeweled third-eye winked up at him. "I'll have my tea, now," he said firmly, and as the women hastened in the direction of the kitchen, he bent to rescue the headgear. He stroked the soft velvet.

NOTE: *Following is a translation of "Tocado." I wanted you all to see what the Sephardic language, called Ladino, looks like. This language, which many Sephardic families still use, has become more archaic over the centuries. The language was spoken in Spain and when the Sephardim left their homes in Spain and wandered far away, they carried their language with them. There are great differences in vocabulary; depending on what country a family lived in. My husband Joe, whose family lived for many generations in Turkey, and a good friend of ours, Daisy Williamson, whose family lived in Thessalonica, used to have a wonderful time arguing over words and whose choice was correct. Many consider the language a dead one, and yet, how can this be, when the language is still being used?*

What fascinates me is that when my story, "Tocado," was printed in the journal, Aki Jerusalem, the editor sent copies to me and I leafed through the pages and didn't even recognize my own story until I noticed my name underneath "El Tocado!"

El Tokado

(trenzladado del Inglez por Alegra Amado)

Djoya ni lo avia visto al prinsipio. Paresia tanto a los otros ombres ke se paseavan kon un ayre de importansia en la estasion de tren de Izmir. Sonriyo. David estava deviniendo de dia en dia mas evropeo en su aparensia. Paresia a un fransez o a un italiano. El vestido ke vestia era tan diferente de lo ke se lluviera vestido unos kuantos anyos atras...

Djoya se asento, en la mizma manera ke simpre, los djinoyos apegados, los pies formando un triangulo i las manos sovre sus piernas. Tenia la kavesa alta i estava observando a la djente de manera alerta, kon sus ojos grizos. En akeyos dias la vida en Turkia se estava trokando rapidamente, en los ke los komersantes i las figuras politikas estavan siendo enfluensadas mas i mas por los paizes oksidentales.

Kuando su marido David se le aserko, se saludaron kon la formalidad adekuada a una mujer i su marido ke se enkontran en publiko. Djoya avia pasado un buen dia en el sentro, vijitando a sus ermanas i estava dainda basho la enfluensa del dia agradable ke avia pasado. Estava kaminando kon orgolio, i estava konsiente del fakto ke su vestimienta reflektava un sierto estatuo finansial i cultural. Vestia una jaketa de brokar bordada de samara. Komo munchas mujeres sefaradis a los prinsipios de los anyos 1900, Djoya tambien vestia esta jaketa en lugar del mas moderno manto ke la mayoria de la mujeres evropeas vestian. I en lugar de tapar sus kaveyos kon una peruka komo azian las mujeres eshkenazis, eya tenia un tokado o sea se avia tapado sus ermozos kaveyos pretos kon un tokado de velur ke tenia una grande brocha i en medio una piedra presioza ke paresia un treser ojo.

Djoya i su marido entraron a un vagon de segunda klasa, ke no estava enteramente yeno. Djoya metio sus paketos ariva i se asento de una menera ke indikava a su marido ke le esta apartando un lugar especial a su lado. Ma en lugar de asentarse, David se kedo en pies de manera silensioza. Avrio la boka para avlar. Djoya lo miro kon ojos ke preguntavan.

"Djoya, me vo asantar kon algunos de mis konosidos en el vagon de primera klasa." Le amostro su bilieto para provar sus palavras.

Djoya avrio la boka en sorpreza. "Ma, David, - disho, siempre mos asentamos djuntos kuando viajamos en treno."

"Si, ma...bueno..."

Djoya se alevanto rapidamente i se estiro para tomar sus paketos.

"No, mi mujer," disho el.

"Ke bovedad" respondio eya kon ravia silensioza. "Merka simplemente un bilieto de primera klasa para mi i viajare djuntos kon ti i tus konosidos. De kuando es ke empesates tu a viajar en primera klasa?"

David respondio de manera no muy klara. "Mmm, ultimamente. Mis kologas evropeos vijan en primera klasa i...Lo importante es el lavoro." Se dio kuento ke los kompartamentos del treno se estavan inchendo. "Devo irme sino va pedrer mi lugar." Se le aserko i le kareso la mano. "El viaje no es largo" Disho kon boz basha." Vamos a kaminar endjuntos de la estasion de treno a kaza.

Djoya kedo mirando la espalda de su marido kon su perfecto vestido. Su marido se transformo en supito en un ajeno. Su tension se estava notando en su kuerpo.

La djente ke estava viajando en el mizmo vagon ke eya la estava mirando kon kuriozidad, fasinada a la vista por el kurto interkambio de palavras entre eya i su marido. Djoya konsintio umiliasion. Keria azerse ainda mas chika de lo ke era fizilamente i mizmo devenir invizible.

Miro a sus manos ke estavan serradas enpunyos. Izo esforsos para avrir sus manos i empeso a observar sus palmas en las kualas eran tan klaros los sinyos de muncho lavoro. Kon todas sus kriaturas, i los echos de kaza ke devia azer...ke se podia esperar?

Asta agora, avia konsentido muncha satisfaksion de su vida

yena de lavoro i aktividad: de su grande famiya ke bivia en kaza, inkluyendo a vezes viejas tias o primas ermanas ke no eran kazadas i ke no tenian onde bivir; del gizado i de su lavoro kon la shastra ke venia periodikamente para kuzir vistidos a todos los de kaza. Malgrado ke las ijas grandes ya podian ayudar en la kuzina, i ke la mas grande de eyas era enkargada de la importante mission de yevar el pan al orno local, avia tanto ke azer! Malgrado toto esto, siempre de yevar el pan al orno tokal, avia tanto ke azer! Malgrado todo esto, siempre penso ke tenia mazal, ke su kazamiento era una aliansa de 2 personas ke eran iguales. Djoya suspiro demuevo. Le empeso a tuyir la kavesa.

El treno estava entrando a la estasion de Burnabat, sus estasion. Djoya se alevanto kon dinyidad, arekojo sus paketos i aspero. Savia ke era possible ke la estavan mirando i por esto salio del vagon kon la kavera alta. David ya la estava asperando abasho ma, sin azer atension, el se torno verso sus muevos amigos para dizirles unas kuantas palavras.

Jeneralmente Djoya uviera asperado ke David le aga sinyo ke esta pronto a empesar a kaminar verso sus kaza ma esta vez el fakto ke se torno a aviar kon sus amigos, fue simplemente el kolmo. Djoya lo desho en la estasion i empeso a kaminar sola. Estava adelantando tan rapidamente ke eya mizma estava sorprendida.

Yego a la entrada de su kaza. Su ija grande, Kadem, aparesio en la puerta i le pregunto kon sorpresa: "Ma, onde esta el papa?"

Djoya no endenyo mizmo responder, simplemente mostro kon su kavera la direksion de la estasion, indikando ke su marido estava yegando.

Kadem se travo para permeter ke su madre entre al kurtijo. Apronto el kafe i aspero ke su madre se asente konfortablemente. "Mama kontame, ke paso?" le pregunto i Djoya le konto su experiensa tan umiliante kon una boz ke estava tremblando kon ravia. "I entonses," adjusto, kon kalmo finalmente, "estava tan araviada kon el, ke refuzi mizmo ke me akompanye a kaza."

Kadem observo a su madre kon penserio. "Mama, saves kual es el problema?"

Djoya devino tensa. "Problema? De ke problema avlas? Lo ke se yo, es ke fui insultada i umiliada."

"Mama," apunto Kadem kon pasensia. "Tu problema es ke sos muy a la vieja." Se kedo unos kuantos momentos para karesarle sus kaveyos peynados tan ermozos antes de kontinuar. "El mundo se esta trokando tan rapidamente. Mizmo la Turkie se esta trokando. Tu no estas adelantando kon el tiempo. El papa si esta adelantando."

"Ke kere dizir, adelantar kon el tiempo?" disho Djoya. "Yo me visto bien, siempre me veo bien, no?"

Kadem dezaparesio por un minuto i retorno kon un espejo oval. "Mira, mirate."

Djoya examino su imajen. "I...entonses?" disho finalmente.

Entones," disho Kadem. "Te tapas tus marviozos kaveyos kon este trapo a la vieja. Te vistes una jaketa ordinaria en lugar de un muevo manto largo de Paris..."

Djoya la interrumpio. "Visto la vertimienta de una mujer tradisionala sefardi. Komo mi mama antes de mi."

Si, i tu marido se esta averguensando de ti. No kijo viajar en el mizmo vagon kon ti. Prefere asentarse kon tos evropeos modernos.

Djoya avrio sus manos en dezespero. "Ma, ke puedo azer yo?"

La repuesta de Kadem estava pronta. "Esto es lo ke puedes azer." Kito lo ke su madre tensa sovre la kavesa koza ke te metes sovre la kavera. Deshame arreglarlo." Kito un peyne i empeso a peynar las buklas naturalas de Djoya. En mirandose en la espejo, Djoya empeso a soniryir.

Kadem kontinuo a lavorar i adjusto: "Kuando terminamos kon tus kaveyos, vamos a avlar de un muevo manto de Paris."

Djoya avrio la boka para protestar, ma no disho nada. Kontinuo a mirar kon fasinansion su imajen ke se estava trokando.

La transformasion de Djoya se estava kompletando en lo ke David entro de la puerta, akompanyado por la djoven Mathilde. Avia enkontrado a sus ija chika ke estava saliendo de la eskola. "Oh, mama, estas tan ermoza!" grito la ijika interrumpiendo a Djoya i a Kaddem ke se estavan riyendo. Kadem estava al lado de Djoya ke estava asantado kon un ayre orgoliozo. Sovre la chika meza al lado de eya, avia jurnales kon fotografias de los mas modernos mantos.

Kadem miro a su padre. "Papa," disho, "los ombres no son los unikos ke pueden trokarsen. Mozotros, las mujerees tambien mos podemos trokar." Tomo el tocado de la pierna de su madre i lo echo embasho. "Mama – disho eya - mas no deves viajar en Segunda klasa."

David miro a su mujer i a su ija i despues al tocado embasho. "Agora kero mi kafe," disho firmemente i en lo ke las mujeres se fueron a la kuzina, se aboko para tomar el tocado de enbasho i kareso el velur suave.

Cadem in New York

Cadem helped Ezra into his suit coat and kissed him goodbye. She blew him another kiss from the door of the new apartment and listened until the click-clack of his hard-soled shoes could be heard no more. They had married in Smyrna, then made the journey by boat to America. It had taken them some time to settle into their apartment, and this was to be Ezra's first day back at work.

Running to the window, she waved as her husband crossed the street to catch the Ninth Avenue El. Once up the escalator, he would drop his nickel in the slot, pass through the turnstile, mount the stairs, and reappear on the platform directly opposite the apartment window. She waited. Seeing him, she waved once more. He clutched his chest, pretending exhaustion, then laughed.

"Oh, Ezra, I love you," she said, blowing a final kiss as the train drowned her small voice. Her hands over her ears, she watched him board the noisy black monster that would carry him to his office.

As the train disappeared, she turned from the window. There was so much to do. But even as she washed the dishes, the silence of their tiny apartment settled about her, and she missed her family, so far away, across the ocean. Defiantly humming a tune, she began to sweep the floor, but her movement became slower and slower until she stopped. She sat down. "What is wrong?" she wondered. She put her face in her hands, not crying, just sitting, feeling sad.

Then she shook herself. "Don't be silly. You're just used to having Ezra around and miss him." She resumed her work but began weeping as she swept.

It wasn't Ezra she was missing just now, but her family—her sisters and her parents, who were far from New York. How she missed them all, especially her sisters, for they had always done the housework together, joking and singing as they worked, with Mama sometimes coming into the room and laughing too.

Cadem began to pace. Back and forth, back and forth, only a few steps in any direction, for the room was small. She felt smothered. Only this morning it had seemed such a wonderful apartment, but now she hated it. It was so little and so far from the ground. And the trains were so loud! She clapped her hands over her ears as one thundered past.

She began to dust the furniture, then flinging down the cloth, she ran to the window. Her head spun as she looked down. How different this apartment was from her home back in Turkey. But apartments were scarce in New York City, and they had only gotten this one through a stroke of luck.

Cadem sighed. Money—there was a problem. At home she and her sisters never used to worry. Whenever they wanted something, they had only to ask Papa and he would always say yes, after grumbling a little. But Ezra had told her that now she would have to buy the food and spend only a tiny amount, pay the rent, and all sorts of things. Just thinking about it gave her a headache. She shrugged. No matter how gloomy she might feel there was still work to be done. She picked up the cloth and began again.

Groaning sounds came from the dumbwaiter. She hurried into the kitchen, picked up the trash and ran to the dumbwaiter shaft. She knew what to do, for Ezra had explained how the superintendent each day raised the dumbwaiter so that the occupants might rid themselves of their trash. Excitedly, she peered down. They had nothing so wonderful as this in Smyrna! She could see the dumbwaiter box rising slowly, squeaking and rumbling, and she knew the superintendent must be pulling at the ropes.

The turbaned head of a woman appeared suddenly in the opening below.

"*Buenos días,*" said Cadem without thinking, then she switched quickly to "hello," singing it out, as she was so glad to see someone.

The woman looked up. "Oh, hello. You're new here, aren't you?"

"Yes," said Cadem. "Only a week are we moved here."

To this the woman said, "No, I mean you're a foreigner, just moved to this country."

Cadem nodded.

"Thought so," said the woman. "You don't act like you belong here. You're too friendly."

And when Cadem didn't say anything, the woman added, "You'd better be careful, shouldn't go around speaking to strangers and smiling at people."

Cadem began to feel frightened, as the woman went on. "I'll warn you, in New York it's not safe to speak to people you don't know. Can't tell what they might be up to. And don't ever smile at a stranger. Murderers and thieves, you know."

Just then the dumbwaiter reached the woman's level, and Cadem couldn't see her any more. She waited for it to rise to her level, set the rubbish carefully within it, and watched the dumbwaiter lower slowly back down the shaft.

Cadem withdrew and sat huddled in a chair. What a terrible country, she thought. Well, I won't stay. I'll go home. And she went on for a long time thinking such thoughts, knowing all the time she couldn't go home, for she had a husband to take care of. She sat thinking about all the dreadful things that could happen to her, while trains thundered into and out of the station.

Suddenly Cadem looked at the clock and realized she would have to go shopping for dinner. "I can't!" she thought, frightened. And she curled up in a chair. But she forced herself up, knowing that groceries have to be bought, and husbands fed.

With a defiant air she changed into one of her best dresses. Taking from her hatbox her prettiest straw hat, the one with flowers, she set it square on her head. She picked up her little purse and walked to the door of the apartment.

There her courage vanished. She had to force herself to open the door and go out, expecting to be attacked by mobs of villains. She walked down the six flights and out into the sunshine. She advanced down the street with head held high. Proud she looked from without, but she was much frightened within, for there were many people on the street, and she was certain they were all thieves and murderers. Chin high, she passed them all, determined that if she were to die, she would do so bravely. She never knew that many looked after her, for she was quite beautiful.

She forced herself to enter one of the little shops and made her purchases, speaking up bravely to the storekeeper and wrinkling her brow as she paid for her groceries in the unfamiliar American money. Outside, Cadem sighed as she looked at the piles of fruits and vegetables, dejected and wilted from the heat of the day. She picked up a peach and looked at it sadly, remembering the lovely peaches at home.

"Peaches are terrible this year, aren't they?" asked a voice in her ear, and Cadem jumped, on guard against strangers. But she relaxed when she saw the plump little woman next to her, holding a melon up to her nose and smelling it. This could be no thief or murderer, thought Cadem, so she smiled shyly at her.

Just then the shopkeeper came out and frowned at the ladies for handling his produce. Frightened again, Cadem scuttled away, until she remembered herself and began walking straight and proud once again. Marching bravely onward, parcel in hand, past all the people, all the potential thieves and murderers, out of the sunlight into the gloom of the apartment building. She climbed the six flights, fumbling about for the key.

Safe in the refuge of her apartment, Cadem set down her packages and collapsed weakly onto the sofa. She felt as if she had fought a war all alone. She lay there, alternately pitying and admiring herself, until she saw that she was wrinkling her good dress. As she went into the bedroom and changed, she thought about the lady with the melon.

"She wasn't afraid," Cadem thought. "She wasn't afraid to speak to strangers." She walked slowly into the tiny kitchen, thinking about the bravery of the lady, and wondering how she herself could summon together the courage to walk on the street again tomorrow.

She put the groceries away, clucking her tongue at the cost. She could get much nicer vegetables from the garden back home. But she forgot her troubles in the excitement of getting dinner ready. This, too, was something she'd never done alone before. As she worked, she would run to the window each time she heard a train come in.

After many trains had come and gone, and she had burned a finger and broken a dish, she saw Ezra waving to her from the platform. In a moment he reappeared briefly on the street, waving at her. She hurried about the tiny apartment, putting away the unused mop and broom, lighting the Friday night candle, and looking about the cozy rooms with satisfaction. She flew to the doorway where she could hear the familiar click-clacking up the many flights. Her face shone as she stretched out her arms to greet her husband, her brave husband who was not afraid of thieves and murderers.

Homecoming

The sun shone brightly upon the clumps of people standing on the Turkish shore waiting for the steamer to come into the harbor. Papa stood looking toward the waters, holding Mary, their youngest child, by the hand while Mama talked with a neighbor. Mathilde was playing nearby with some friends. It was a June day in the early 1900s, and the parents were awaiting the arrival of their married daughter, Cadem, who was coming from America for a visit.

"Papa," said Mary, "is it true what they say about my sister Cadem?"

"Is what true, dear," he said absently, staring off over the blue waters.

"That she married a bandit over in America and he was shot to death and that is why she is coming back to us in Smyrna?"

"Of course not," he said. He looked out at the Bay of Smyrna once again, shading his eyes from the sunlight with his hand. "I do not know where all this nonsense about Ezra's being a bandit comes from. All the neighbors are talking about it. You met Cadem's husband once yourself, did you not? Did he look like a bandit?"

"The child hesitated, thinking. "No," he said. "But then I have never seen a bandit."

Her father did not answer and after a bit the child sighed and imitatively placed a hand over her own eyes and looked seaward.

Some moments later Mathilde began jumping up and down. "I see it," she cried. "The boat! It's coming!" And she detached herself from the group of children and ran panting over to her father.

"Mathilde," he said sharply. "Why can't you be a good girl like Mary and wait quietly?"

Mathilde hung her head, but only for a moment.

"Papa?" she blurted out. "Will Cadem wear big golden earrings?" And as her father looked confused, she added, "like the gypsies?"

"Earrings? Like the gypsies?" asked her father. "But why should she?"

"Why? Because her husband is a bandit, at least everyone says so, and gypsies are bandits," said the child looking at her father with big eyes.

Some children standing nearby giggled and whispered, and then looked flustered when they saw Papa looking at them. They all had flushed faces and shiny, excited eyes, and Papa could see that they were hopeful that all sorts of bandits and gypsies would be getting off the boat. He smiled at them as a sort of compensation for having scolded his daughter. He felt Mathilde pulling at his coat and turned to look down at her and smile also. Then he turned again to watch the tiny speck of a boat far out on the horizon. Again he felt a tugging, and remembered that he had not answered Mathilde's questions.

Papa put an arm about her and said, "My child, do not be so foolish as to believe what everyone says." And turning to a fellow villager standing nearby, he began explaining to him what he had already told the children two or three times.

"Cadem," he said, "wrote to us that her husband Ezra was going to spend a few months in a city in America called St. Louis. This is quite far from New York City where they live and it is very hot in summer, so Cadem decided to come home to visit us. Ezra too, she told us, is going to come here in a few months. But for some reason our friends have made up their minds that she married badly and that is why she is coming home." He shrugged. "Oh well, I suppose they must gossip about something."

The boat was growing bigger and coming closer. Puffs of dark smoke arose from the stack. Mama stopped chatting with her neighbor and she drew closer to Papa and the two girls. Automatically, Mama smoothed Mary's rumpled hair and straightened Mathilde's shirtwaist, without taking her eyes from the boat.

"David," said Mama, "do you really think that Cadem gave her true reasons for coming home? Do you think that Ezra could be in trouble somehow?"

"Joya!" How could you think that?" exclaimed Papa in a shocked voice. He took out his handkerchief and mopped his brow, although the day was not hot.

He squinted his eyes, trying to see Cadem on the boat.

"Mathilde, my child," said Papa after a few minutes, "those children you were playing with, are they not the children of our village?"

"Yes, Papa."

"Are they perhaps meeting friends or relatives coming off the boat?" Papa asked.

"I don't know," said Mathilde. "They said they were here because their parents are here."

"Oh?" he said. Then suddenly jovial, he added, "Probably they brought the children down especially to see the boat come in. It is exciting, isn't it, children?" And he took his hat in his hands, and holding it by the rim absently turned it round and round.

"Mama," he said, "I saw you talking with Mrs. Bensousane. Is she meeting relatives here on the boat?"

"No," said Mama. "I thought that too, but when I asked she looked embarrassed and mumbled something about just happening to be here."

The boat came nearer, and people began crowding down toward the water's edge. They were not yet close enough to identify passengers, so everyone was waving.

"Joya," said her husband, still squinting. "Has it occurred to you that a lot of people are here today?"

"You mean from our village?"

"Yes," said Papa. "I think half the village is here on this shore."

She hesitated. "I think," she said finally, "they have come down to see Cadem."

"How silly!" said Papa looking at her. "Why would they want to do that?"

Mama looked at him. He turned back to the water.

Aboard ship, people were shouting and waving hellos to those on shore. Those on shore were waving back. All the children were jumping up and down. Somewhere a band was playing.

A sailor aboard the boat tossed to a man on the dock a piece of rope, which was made fast. The boat bumped against the dock and another rope was tied. Then the gangplank was let down and passengers began to disembark.

Mama and Papa stood close together as streams of people flowed from the boat. Fortuna and Mathilde watched curiously. People coming down the gangplank were greeted by relatives with glad shouts.

Minutes passed and the stream of people coming from the boat slowed and finally stopped. Mama clutched Papa by the arm. Her hand was cold.

"Where is Cadem, Papa?" she asked.

Papa didn't answer. He just stood there listening to everyone laughing and shouting and the band playing. He became aware that people from the village were looking at them. He managed to smile at Mama, and they reached out and pulled the two children closer to them.

There was a sudden hush in the laughter and shouting as a fashionably dressed, black-haired girl walked alone down the gangplank, followed by three porters carrying her luggage. She stopped to talk with a customs inspector.

"What a lovely hat," Papa heard a girl near him say.

"Oh, what a beautiful taffeta jacket," said another girl.

"It's a maternity jacket," the girl's mother informed her dryly.

"Her hands! Look how they sparkle! They are covered with rings," gasped another girl.

"It's Cadem, grown fat," shrieked Mathilde, and she ran forward, followed by Mary.

Mama and Papa stared hard at Cadem. Suddenly they both began to look very happy.

"Papa!"

"Mama!"

Speaking together, they started to laugh. "We're going to be grandparents!"

"With her wearing such fine clothes, Ezra must surely be doing very well," said Mama. "We were foolish to have worried."

"I worry?" Papa laughed loudly. "I did not worry." Then he clutched at Mama's arm. "Joya, my knees are weak."

"Well, I have been worried ever since we received Cadem's letter. And I mentioned it to Mrs. Bensousane and she said maybe things were not going well with Ezra. But it was all very foolish. We should not have worried. If only Cadem had told me she was with child!"

And Papa smiled to himself, for now he understood. Mama had dropped a thread of doubt to Mrs. Bensousane as to why Cadem was coming home, and from there Mrs. Bensousane had picked up the thread and tossed it to neighbors and so on, until the fantastic stories had been woven into a tapestry about bandits and shootings and gypsies.

The customs inspector was now finished with Cadem. Papa took Mama by the hand and they hurried forward. Swooping down upon Cadem, they embraced her, then Mathilde and Mary threw their arms about her waist and turned their faces up to be kissed. Proudly Mama and Papa looked at their daughter.

Friends and neighbors were surging forward to say hello and to see her clothes and jewels at close range. Cadem was laughing and crying with joy to see everyone.

"Oh, it is so good to see you all," she said. "America is wonderful, but I will always love home."

Firmly, her father took her by one arm and her mother by the other, and walking tall and straight and beaming at everyone they led her over to the carriage. The three of them sat up in front and Mary and Mathilde scrambled into the back, which was piled high with luggage.

"Cadem, why didn't you tell us?" asked Mama, looking at the maternity jacket with reproachful eyes.

"I was afraid you would worry, Mama."

"Worry?" said Papa. "Worry! You should hear what we have been through with the neighbors since we told them you were coming home." And he laughed to show that he wasn't really angry.

They looked down and saw that a group of people had followed them and were standing on both sides of the carriage. Mama and Papa and Cadem sat in the front and the two little girls in the back, all stiffly erect, trying to act like royalty, but beaming. Papa spoke to the horse, which began stepping forward smartly along the road leading home, while a group of disgruntled villagers who had hoped for bandits and gypsies looked on in disappointment.

A Bird in a Cage

"Goodbye. Do have a pleasant afternoon. No, that is quite all right. I'll enjoy spending the afternoon here. No, I assure you it is a pleasure."

Mathilde, now 15, and visiting in New York City, waved to her father and to Mr. and Mrs. Schenasi once again before turning from the doorway. Catching in the great gilded mirror a glimpse of herself wearing her long yellow dress, she paused for a moment to admire her reflection. She moved across to one of the tall windows, where she stood looking down through bars of sunlight at the people leaving the house.

A shiny car stood at the curb, with a uniformed man holding open the door. She saw Mrs. Schenasi climb in, then Papa and Mr. Schenasi. How different Papa looked without his Turkish fez! Mathilde could hardly recognize him in the flat straw hat he had purchased immediately upon their arrival in New York. The car started slowly, then stopped. Mr. Schenasi stuck his head out of the window and spoke to the gardener. Finally the car glided smoothly away.

After all the attention she had been given by her hosts, it seemed both peaceful and strangely quiet now that she was alone. For a moment, Mathilde wished she had gone with them instead of waiting at the Schenasi home for delivery of a package. But in another minute she had forgotten this whim. She looked forward to the prospect of spending an afternoon alone in this lovely home. Her eyes sparkled as she surveyed the large room with its heavy, ornately carved furniture and thick wall hangings. Her feet sank deep into the oriental rug as she walked. Mr. Schenasi, who owned the Turkish cigarette factory where Mathilde's brothers, Eli and Moïse worked, had certainly done well in America.

She cranked up the Victrola, put on a record, and began

snapping her fingers and stepping about in time to the music. What fun jazz was, and how she would enjoy showing the dance steps to her sisters when she returned home to Turkey! She and her father had been in New York visiting her brothers for more than a month now, and Papa had not mentioned returning home at all. The record finished, she shut off the machine, and still humming the tune and snapping her fingers, she danced about the room. She paused before the canary cage and smiled. She peered through the bars at him and whistled, or at least tried to whistle. "Whe, Whe! Hello, little canary, hello, you sweet thing." And she waggled a finger at him. The canary awoke, retreated to the other side of his cage and looked at her resentfully.

Mathilde laughed with pleasure and shook her finger at him. What a pretty little bird. At home they had always had many dogs and cats, but never a bird. As she thought of home, she suddenly became homesick and felt a lump in her throat.

Wiping her eyes and laughing at herself for crying, Mathilde remembered that Mrs. Schenasi had said something about giving the bird a bath. Mathilde wondered how one gave a bird a bath, and then decided she could follow the same procedure she had often used in bathing dogs and babies at home. Only the birdbath she would do on a smaller scale.

She ran lightly out of the room, singing as she went, and returned shortly, holding daintily a small bowl filled with sudsy water. Lifting down the canary cage, Mathilde set it on a table and opened wide the cage door. The little bird sat quite still, as Mathilde gently wrapped her fingers about his delicate body. She set the bird down in the midst of the suds and with great care began washing him. She noticed suddenly that he had become quite limp, and, frightened, she lifted him from the suds and set him on the table. He did not move.

"Oh I've killed him," she thought and laid her head down upon the shiny surface of the table.

After a few moments of remorse she raised her head. "He's not dead, he's still breathing," and swiftly she picked him up and placed him on a heavy, upholstered chair in the warm sunlight. Perhaps the heat of the sun would make him feel better.

In her hurry to lift the bird from his bath she had spilled water on the table. She jumped up and ran into the kitchen for a towel. Back she came, towel clutched in her hand, and she stood looking at the little wet bird. With his feathers flattened down from the water, he looked about half his normal size.

"How tiny and helpless he looks," she thought. "Is he still breathing?" she asked herself in sudden panic, and bent close to reassure herself. He was, and she felt so encouraged at this that she began to wipe from the mahogany table the pool of soapy water.

Once more she placed herself close to the canary, and this time his breathing seemed stronger. "I had better put him in his cage," she thought. "He'll probably feel more secure if he wakes up there." And she set the cage down beside the bird.

The canary awoke and, blinking his eyes, remained motionless for a moment. Then, shaking himself, he spread his stubby wings and headed for an open window.

"Oh, no!" thought Mathilde, as she watched helplessly.

As the canary neared the window, the sound of a whirring lawnmower down below startled the bird, and he banked abruptly and began flying along one wall of the room.

Mathilde closed the window and heaved a sigh of relief. She looked about for the bird, which was comfortably seated high on a golden picture frame.

"You naughty bird!" she scolded aloud. "You ungrateful thing, you. I saved your life and now you are there on that picture where I can't get at you." Then she laughed aloud for joy that the bird was not dead, and at herself scolding the bird for not being grateful she hadn't killed him.

Mathilde drew a chair over to a spot just beneath the picture, lifted up her skirts with one hand, stepped onto a chair, and stretched high to reach the canary with her free hand. Off he flew, lighting on a chest of drawers on the far side of the room. Mathilde jumped down from the chair and went after him, moving her legs almost as rapidly as he did his wings. She put her hand out to catch him and felt the soft feathers brush against her fingers, but when she looked down at her hand, no bird was to be seen. He was now gazing down at her from a comfortable perching spot on a curtain rod. His feathers had dried and he was once again a fat, fluffy, yellow canary.

Mathilde laughed again. The canary was so fat and sleepy looking, yet he could fly so swiftly through the air. Just then the doorbell rang.

Startled for a moment, Mathilde then remembered that the Schenasis were expecting a package to be delivered. She smoothed her hair, straightened her dress, and went to the door. She opened it just a crack, fearful lest the canary should escape, and took the box, opening the door just wide enough to slip the package through. She thanked the deliveryman politely and shut the door quickly.

Mathilde set down the package and looked about for the canary. Where was he?

"Oh, there you are!" she said aloud. "My, the delivery man looked puzzled. He must have wondered why I didn't open the door wider, and perhaps why I had such a wild look in my eye."

The little canary sat sleepily on top of a table and looked at her. Mathilde began walking stealthily toward him, reaching her hands out slowly as she advanced. He flew away rapidly, chirping as he went, and settled on a door molding.

"Oh, what shall I do?" Mathilde cried in vexation. "I'll never catch him. I can't sprout wings, so he will always be able to escape me. He's much too high now. I couldn't reach him even from a chair."

As she said this, the little ball of yellow fluff glided downward and alighted atop a heavily ornamented lamp in the center of the room.

Mathilde dashed over, but by the time she reached the lamp, the bird was on the far side of the room, flying lazily about.

"Oh, you silly bird," scolded Mathilde again. "I had such lovely plans for the afternoon. I was going to read, I wanted to play the piano, I was going to gather a bouquet from the garden for Mrs. Schenasi, and all sorts of things. And now I have to spend my afternoon chasing you up and down." And she stretched up her hands to catch the bird, but he was flying too high.

Up and down the room the bird and the girl in the yellow dress went all that afternoon. The canary seemed never to tire, but poor Mathilde would at times flop exhausted into a chair. Always, whenever this happened, the canary would fly quite close to her and, with renewed energy, she would spring up and give chase.

The sunlight coming into the room grew paler as the day slipped away. The tall clock in the corner struck slowly, five times, and following that, the engine of an automobile was heard coming up the driveway.

Mathilde started. She hadn't realized it was getting so late. For a moment she contemplated flight into the garden, in order to avoid the embarrassment of having to explain the empty cage and the bird flying about the room. But she rejected this thought as being childish, and stood by the door waiting to hear footsteps on the stairway. When the footsteps had grown loud and she could hear the voices of Papa and the Schenasis, she opened the door a crack and peered out.

When Papa saw his daughter's flushed face looking solemnly at him from behind the slit in the door, he stopped talking and laughing and looked worried. The Schenasis, too, ceased to laugh and looked puzzled.

"What is it, my daughter?" asked Papa gently. "Did someone come and frighten you?"

She shook her head and beckoned them to come in. Silently they filed into the room one after the other, going sideways, as Mathilde did not open the door very far. Once inside, Mathilde quickly shut the door, and then she began to laugh at their solemn faces.

"I didn't mean to frighten you," she said. "It's the bird." And she pointed at the canary. "He got out of the cage. I was giving him a bath and almost killed him. And then after he lay in the sunlight for a while, he almost flew out the window. And I have been trying to get him back in the cage but cannot catch him. I am so sorry, Mrs. Schenasi." All this she said in one breath. Papa was relieved and began looking more cheerful. Mrs. Schenasi laughed.

"Poor Mathilde," she said. "I should have told you that you

don't *give* a bird a bath, you let him take it himself. You could have just put the bowl in his cage and he would have managed quite well." She paused, and then laughed a little more, but kindly, when she saw the bowl of suds still lying on the table. "And *not* with soap, Mathilde dear."

"Oh?" said Mathilde.

Then Mr. Schenasi spoke. "I guess we also should have told you, Mathilde," he said, looking with mock severity at his wife, "that we often let the canary out of the cage. We have found that he will always go back in when he becomes hungry."

"It really is too bad," said Mrs. Schenasi, beginning to have difficulty holding back her ripples of laughter, "that you had to spend your afternoon chasing the bird."

"Oh," said Mathilde, and for a moment she appeared to be on the borderline between tears of embarrassment and laughter at her own foolishness. Then as she saw the older people circled around her, looking at her with love, she laughed too, and her laughter rang out joyously in the long narrow room.

Symphony 1912

Mathilde walked down the street looking into shop windows and at people surging past her. Down the street came a clanging of bells and the pounding of horses' hooves. She stood with others on the curb as the great white horses pulling the fire wagon hurtled past, swerving wildly from side to side, just missing two men still in the street and then disappearing into the coming dusk.

Mathilde watched until she could see the wagon no longer, and then walked on. She turned in at the red brick building, which said on its front "School for Adult Education," and began climbing the steep steps. She pushed open the door and entered the school, leaving the darkness behind her.

As she walked down the long hallway, she could hear the sounds of many languages spoken by other students at the night school, and her ears liked the sounds. She was reminded of musical instruments tuning for a concert. There, leaning against the wall, were the violins—Chinese girls sing-songing in high sweet voices; in an opposite corner were the bass viols—a group of German youths communicating in deep vibrating tones; and in a doorway were the woodwinds—a Frenchman speaking like a flute, rapidly and with many pauses and running up and down the scale with his sentences; and an Italian, sounding like an oboe as he spoke in a melodic and reedy voice.

Mathilde opened the classroom door and entered. It was early and the teacher had not yet come. She sat down quickly. In a few moments the teacher came in, and everyone straightened and looked at him respectfully. He was a thin man, very tall, with bushy eyebrows. He reminded Mathilde of pictures she had seen of Abraham Lincoln.

She was so happy that she was enrolled in this course. When her father, who had brought her to America, left to return to Turkey, he had suggested that she might want to study English.

"We will not let you stay here forever," he had said, "but your brothers and their wives would like to have you here with them for a while. Be helpful to them whenever you can, and try to keep on learning. English would be a good language to master."

And Mathilde had taken her father's advice. She loved learning a new language, and she enjoyed living with her older brother Eli and his wife, who had a new baby, just as she also enjoyed spending much time with Moïse and his wife. She was happy in New York although she did get homesick at times.

"Tonight," said the teacher, "I would like to have us begin to use the English language in order to help us get acquainted with one another. We have been studying long enough for you to be able to speak it, and now I think you should begin to use it."

He paused to give the class an opportunity to digest his words, and then spoke again. "You come from different countries and you speak different languages. But now that you are learning a common language, you can begin to use this language and learn about one another. Would anyone volunteer to sit before the class and answer questions as to where he came from and what his home country is like?"

Mathilde puzzled for a moment over the meaning of "volunteer," then having decided what he meant, raised her hand. The teacher smiled, and she went up front and seated herself, arranging her long skirts primly, then sat blushing, with her head down.

"I will begin with the first question," said the professor. "Where are you from?"

"Mathilde looked at him and then at the class. They were all sitting and looking at her. She blushed harder, until she felt so warm she half expected to hear the horses pounding down the street again, dragging the wagon behind them to put her out. She could not remember a word of English! She stared at her hands, wondering what had made her raise one of them in the first place. Then she looked up at the class again, and this time she almost laughed. They looked so worried for her! She didn't have to be afraid. How silly for her to have been afraid.

The words in English came, and she said:

"I come from Smyrna." And she listened to the words as they came from her lips. She had practiced speaking at home, but this was different. This was real, not practice. It was beautiful.

But the faces before her looked blank, so she added, pronouncing each word slowly and carefully:

"It is in Turkey."

The students smiled as they listened to the words and they nodded to one another, for they knew where Turkey was.

The professor smiled at Mathilde and then encouragingly at the class. Under the spell of this smile a dark-eyed girl rose and, blushing too, asked Mathilde a question.

"How . . . many . . . of . . . brothers . . . and sisters . . . are . . . . you?" She spoke very slowly, each word coming forth as a distinct entity from her lips, and the class listened and weighed with their own lips. An awed look came over the girl's face as she spoke, and Mathilde knew she too was feeling the magic of speaking the new language.

Everyone nodded approvingly as the girl finished and then turned to Mathilde. But in her enthusiasm for the sounds of the language, she had forgotten to investigate the meaning, and the class twitched nervously for her while Mathilde thought over the words. Oh yes, how many brothers and sisters did she have? *Dos brothers*, she almost said aloud, but stopped herself in time. *Ocho*—what was the English for that? And she counted to herself, moving her fingers, one, two, three . . . eight, that was it!

"Two of the brothers and eight of the sisters," said Mathilde, and the faces before her nodded and lost the worried look and smiled to one another. All except for the girl, who now looked disappointed. Perhaps she had hoped to brag of her large family?

Now a gray-haired woman was asking, "The city, did you live in the city?" and her face too changed as she heard the sound of herself speaking the new language.

"No," said Mathilde. "We lived . . ." and she had to pause here to think out the phrases…"in the country. We had a big house and much land around her." She waved her arms. Her eyes shone now and she looked at the class, eager for more questions.

A young man stood up, and looking at the teacher nervously, fired at Mathilde in a loud voice,

"How many wives has your father?"

And he sat down abruptly, looking worried, for he was not certain he should have asked the question, but also looking hard at Mathilde, waiting for an answer.

"One," said Mathilde. "We live in Turkey, yet we are not Turkish. Of Arabs and Muslims you are thinking."

"Oh?" said the boy, in a not quite convinced tone of voice.

And Mathilde laughed aloud, for their conversation had made the faces before her turn first to the boy and then to herself, and she was reminded of a tennis game she had once seen where the faces had also bobbed first in one direction, then in another.

Someone was speaking. "You are French like myself, *n'est-ce pas?*" said a girl with short black hair and bangs cascading over her forehead.

"No," said Mathilde smiling. "Many times people think I'm French, because I speak with the accent. But this is because the school I attended in Turkey (*L'Alliance Française*) was a French school. We spoke also the French."

As Mathilde finished speaking, she thought over the sentences and wondered where all the words had come from. She hadn't realized she knew so many, and could say them so fast.

"Of what country are you then," asked the French girl, "if you are not French?"

"My people came from Spain. But that was long ago. Many hundreds of years ago when it was Inquisition."

The boy was on his feet again.

"Your father, how does he dress?"

Again Mathilde laughed, liking the sound of the booming voice. "Like any European," she said. "You are thinking still of the *Arabs.*"

She reached into her handbag. "I have a photograph." The whole class crowded around to see the picture of her family.

"But he looks like anybody," said the boy.

Everyone laughed, and suddenly everyone was talking at

once, telling of their homeland and their families. And the many different people speaking in one tongue, with traces of other tongues, conversed and converged with one another. There was the booming of a drum when the boys spoke and the singing of violins in the words of the women. The voices rose and fell, spoke and were silent, and Mathilde thought it was beautiful to hear.

Later, when class was over and she was again walking down the street, she could remember still the sounds of the voices and the words, and when again she heard the ringing of the bells and the pounding of hooves on the pavement, she did not rush to the curb like the others, but walked dreamily on, past all the shop windows, saying sentences in English to herself.

The Second Annual Ball
at the Club La Luz

Probably at about the same time that my mother-in-law, Mathilde Abraham, and her father David came to America, so also did Rebecca Sides Benforado, with her younger sons, Mark and Maurice. Rebecca had been widowed when her sons were very young; she had taken over the family business and continued to work at the sewing machine. As the world situation worsened and Turkey began conscripting young men for military service, she decided the time had come to take Mark and Maurice to America, following in the steps of the oldest son, Alex.

But the younger sons were not all that she brought to America. In addition to an enormous watermelon tucked under one arm and copper pots dangling from her other hand, Rebecca had by her side Alex's fiancée, Victoria Bensousone. Rebecca had brought her along so that she and Alex might marry and start a family. Rebecca felt that Victoria was a fine young woman, and she did not wish to risk losing her as a daughter-in-law.

At this particular time in history, Sephardic people were pouring into America, with a large number of them settling in New York. Wanting to get to know one another and make suitable choices for marriage, they decided to form a club for young adults. Soon they founded the Club La Luz, a place that could be rented for gatherings and dances by the club members.

We have a framed photograph of that club hanging in our very kitchen. Try to imagine a huge gathering hall with ornate walls. Brilliant clusters of light beam down from the ceiling. The young people who are crammed into the room glow even brighter than the chandeliers. Young women and men, elaborately dressed--the men in tuxedos, the women in gossamer gowns and dainty shoes. Side by side, women and men face the camera bravely, for a photograph of this large group of young Sephardim is about to be taken.

Prominently positioned in the front row, center, is my mother-in-law, Mathilde Abraham, eyes aglow. In her arms she cradles a lovely bouquet of flowers, as do a few of the other young women. Those who are standing in that front row seem to be slightly out of focus down around the feet. But, perhaps the photographer intended this; that fuzzy misty look seems to create the impression that they are already dancing, twirling in the large handsome room.

Somewhat lost in the middle of the crowd is Mark Benforado, the man who would eventually take Mathilde's hand in marriage. And there is a date in the lower left corner of the photograph: *Saturday eve'g, Jan 12th, 1918.* It is the second annual ball of the Club La Luz, being held at the Floral Garden.

Not too long after the festive dance evening, Mark Benforado was inducted into the U.S. Army. This was rather ironic, considering that his mother had brought him all the way across the Atlantic to New York precisely in order to avoid military service in Turkey. However, Mark bravely went off to war, fought in France, and served as the only Turkish soldier in his regiment.

Mathilde, on the other hand, stayed in New York. World War One had broken out in 1914, and although America was not involved, it was not a good time to return to her parents in Turkey. She stayed with various families: for a long time with the Schanasi family, and then later with her brother Eli, his wife Minnie and their two children Leonora and Willie. Eli and Minnie lived in a comfortable apartment, and Mathilde did not mind at all that for a time she shared a crib with Willie. In addition, there was also of course her sister Cadem and her husband and their daughter Fortuna. Sometimes she would live for a while with her other brother Moïse and his wife Mathilde.

And then in April 1917, America got involved in the European War. Although Mathilde and her brothers knew of many young men who were inducted into service, neither of her brothers was called up, probably because they had families to support.

When the war was over and Mark returned again to America, he picked up where he'd left off. He began attending social events at Club La Luz, and ultimately he and Mathilde met. Interestingly, each family had been aware of the existence of the other family while they all still lived in Turkey. Both Mark and Mathilde had attended the *Alliance Française*, although they would have been in different classes. They were instantly attracted to one another.

When Mark's mother, Rebecca, met Mathilde, she too was impressed. She told Mark he must marry Mathilde because she would make him such a fine wife. Rebecca particularly admired the way Mathilde cooked chicken.

And so, finally, Mark and Mathilde married, on September 20, 1920. They took a train to Niagara Falls for their honeymoon, and then settled down to married life in New York City. Rebecca, of course, lived with them. Their first son, Joseph, was born nine months later.

And that is how Mathilde Abraham, that beautiful young woman in the front row of the photograph, became Mathilde Benforado. Let the music begin. May they happily dance the night away.

The Conquering Hero, 1920

Mark patted his stomach contentedly. My, but it was good to be back in New York again. Filled with happiness, he looked about the comfortable surroundings of their small apartment.

Mathilde appeared in the doorway. "Marky, Turkish coffee after your meal?" Without waiting for an answer she carried a tray to the table in front of the sofa and set it down. Sitting beside him, she began pouring.

"Mark," she said. "It's so good to have you back. I was so frightened for you all the time you were gone."

Mark shrugged his narrow shoulders modestly. "It was nothing. You need not have worried."

"But Mark, a war, that's nothing? People get hurt, killed!"

He took a sip of coffee. It was hot and burnt his tongue. He set the cup down.

"You've scarcely told me anything about what happened yet," said Mathilde, "and you've been back for two whole days."

"Mathilde, I'm not sure myself what happened yet. In the past two or three years everything has taken place so rapidly. Just think, over in Smyrna, when we were children, nothing ever happened. Then all of a sudden I was in America, working, going to night school, finding you over here, getting engaged . . ."

At this point Mathilde smiled triumphantly.

He continued, "Next thing I know there is a war, and I am a soldier in it."

"And they took you away from me and sent you across the ocean again," said Mathilde.

"Yes. To France, and all of a sudden there were shootings and bombings, and I was in the middle of it all."

"I know," murmured Mathilde sympathetically. "It must have

been terrible." She paused, hesitating. "But didn't you have any adventures?"

"No, only shootings and bombings," said Mark in a tone of voice which implied he was sorry he didn't since she would have liked him to.

Mathilde took a tiny sip of coffee and squealed, "Ouch, too hot!"

Mark promptly kissed her to make her forget her burnt tongue.

"But, Paris, perhaps?" said Mathilde. "You perhaps saw Paris?"

"No."

"Oh," she said, "I am sure you are really a hero and are just being modest with me."

"No, Mathilde, I am sorry. I would like to be a hero since you would have it so. But I was just a soldier. There were many of us. And war is not nice."

"But surely you must have something to tell me," cried Mathilde impatiently.

Mark looked up at the ceiling, as if hoping to find there an adventure for Mathilde. "No," he said finally, "nothing."

"The boat trip?" she persisted.

"I was sick," he said. "The waves, you know."

"Oh, Mark, there must be something!"

He made wrinkles in his forehead, and thought hard. "Here's a little something which might entertain you," he said. "Mind you," he added quickly, "it's not heroic."

Mathilde clasped her hands and leaned forward in anticipation.

"It all began when . . ." and then he stopped. "Oh, I'm no good at this storytelling."

"Continue your story, Mark," commanded Mathilde, pinching him.

"Well, it happened after a day in which we had partaken of much fighting. I can't talk wisely about that part because I was too busy running here and there shooting and being shot at to describe the battle that was taking place. All day long there were explosions and popping of guns, and I was growing very tired. We were so busy we had had nothing to eat all day long.

"Suddenly I became aware of the fact that with the growing darkness there had come on a kind of quiet. Not that all the shooting had stopped and that we—my platoon, I mean—were the only ones that were shooting. The rest of our battalion had disappeared. We were alone."

Mathilde shivered and drew closer to Mark.

"Somehow we had gotten left behind. A mistake, you know," he continued. "Believe me, Mathilde, it is an extremely peculiar sensation to be fighting when you know that there are about one thousand men fighting along with you, and all of a sudden you look up and find that nine hundred and eighty of the men have disappeared somewhere and there are only some twenty of you left. Right then I felt just like I had coming over on the boat—like my stomach was going up and down instead of standing still."

Mathilde took his hand.

"Well," he said, beginning to tell his story more enthusiastically, "as the others became aware of what had happened, they too stopped shooting. We all gathered in a little group and looked at each other.

"Most of us were privates, but we had one second lieutenant, a college-type fellow. When he saw what had happened, he quickly posted sentries about our little area, and then sat down on the ground to think. He thought awhile, and then he rose rather stiffly and said to us, 'Men, it looks like we've been left behind.' And we nodded our heads. And then he said, 'But I'm sure they'll come back after us tomorrow.' And we nodded our heads hopefully. And then he said, 'Meanwhile, let's see what we have in the way of rations.'

"And then the men who had rations brought them forward and set them down in front of the lieutenant, like he was an idol or something. When all the rations were collected, including any which the sentries had, he looked at it carefully, then said, 'Men, there is before me enough for one meal for only half of you. I would suggest that we draw lots to see which of us eats.'

"The men murmured among themselves, and then one of them produced some matches which he broke up into longs and shorts. He stepped forward and held the handful of matches out to the lieutenant to choose first.

"'No,' said the lieutenant, with chin held high, 'my men I take care of first.'"

"The men looked at him with respect, and then the soldier holding the handful of matches went from man to man. Some grabbed eagerly and cursed when they lost, some drew indifferently, and some did not care at all. When he came round to me, I shook my head and said I did not wish to draw.

"No, Mathilde, it is not that I am a hero. It is just that at home we were taught always that you could not eat happily unless everyone else was eating, and so I did not wish to draw. The other fellows that drew probably did not get taught that at home. And too, they were probably hungrier than I.

"So, I did not eat, but sat and thought about you and my family and my job and the war and would I ever live to see another sunrise. We were all very quiet, for we did not know where the enemy was.

"We could hear occasionally bursting of shells and shooting, but did not know whose they were. We began hearing airplanes overhead, and decided we had better dig holes to sleep in. From time to time we relieved the sentries, I myself being a sentry in the blackest part of night. Very frightening that, Mathilde, peering always into darkness, not knowing what to expect.

"The night passed somehow, without any appearance of the enemy. Morning came and with it, just as the lieutenant had said, came the return of our battalion. They gave us food to eat, and then again like an alarm clock began more shootings and bursting of shells. Our little adventure was over."

"Over?" said Mathilde. "But the shootings?"

"No matter," he said, "I had the occasion to be talking with one of the chaplains, a very nice rabbi, of course. And I happened to tell him my story. He was very interested and asked me when it had taken place, and when I gave him the exact date, what do you think he said, Mathilde? He told me that had been Yom Kippur and that I had done right to fast!"

He leaned forward to taste his coffee. "Mathilde, this coffee is cold."

"Mark dear, I'll get some more right away," she said worshipfully. And she rose and went into the kitchen.

Mark stretched out on the sofa and heaved a contented sigh. My, it was good to be back. And wasn't he lucky his lieutenant hadn't been clever enough to realize that by dividing the rations into tiny portions, everyone could have had a share that lonely night?

My Early Years in Harlem
by
Joseph M. Benforado

The Elevated Train, commonly known as the El, was part of the rail transportation system in New York City. Tracks and cars were supported high in the air, above the city streets, on steel-girdered superstructures, with passenger stations every ten to fifteen city blocks.

I was born in a Harlem apartment in 1921, and at that time the southbound 6th Avenue El had to swerve to the west on 110th Street (6th Avenue being interrupted from 110th to 59th Streets by Central Park) and then turn south again onto 9th Avenue. The station at 110th Street was elevated to the level of the top floor apartments of the buildings facing it. The swerve at 110th Street became known as "Suicide Curve" because of its sad use for that purpose by surely desperate persons. But there was life also, with hordes of people, including my father, taking the El downtown to work. Today, there is no longer a New York City El. It's gone.

And my parents are also gone–they were immigrants who were born in Izmir, Turkey. My grandparents on both sides were Sephardic Jews, whose ancestors had been expelled from Spain about the time of Columbus. Mom and Pop (I never used the terms mother and dad) did not know each other in Izmir and met in New York City, where they learned English. This new language was added to fluency in French and Ladino, old Judeo-Spanish, spoken at home with their families. Pop had served in the U.S. armed forces in France in World War I, then gaining subsequent citizenship. Recall that Turkey, as an ally of Germany, was a belligerent power at the time! Mom became a citizen under postwar legislation, which conferred citizenship on women who married returning doughboys.

Their marriage took place on September 24, 1920 and I was born on June 20, 1921. Mom told me once that Nona, my paternal grandmother, who lived in the apartment with us, had taken notice of her before she and Pop had met. Nona had told Mom, long after the marriage, "Mathilde, when I first saw you, I knew you were the girl I wanted for my Mark."

I was born on the sixth floor at 246 Manhattan Avenue, an apartment house that is still standing. Dr. Reyleah, the family doctor, attended the birth and I assume that while retaining his impressive pince-nez spectacles, he had shed, temporarily, his celluloid collar before welcoming me into the world.

Later, the apartment house at the corner of 110th Street became the center of my world. My father would leave the apartment in the morning by walking down six flights of stairs, only to walk up the same distance to the passenger platform of the El. Then Mom and I would look through the dining room window, which faced 110th Street, to watch for Pop. The platform was level with our floor and when Pop appeared he was so close that in waving to him, I felt as if I could almost touch him.

And through the living room window facing Morningside Avenue, one could gaze down on Morningside Park across the street, above which, on Morningside Heights, loomed the massive medieval-like Cathedral of St. John the Divine. I never entered the structure until 1975 when I attended a medical meeting in New York City. However, my education about non-Jewish aspects of religion came quite early when Mom took me to the apartment of a Christian neighbor to see a decorated Christmas tree.

Morningside Park was my playground. and the most vivid recollection of all its joys is of sitting in a beautiful shining red roadster (a large toy automobile) with a young girl my age, whose car it was. The fun for me was proudly pedaling her up and down the ever curving paths in the park. My next adventure with driving the opposite sex anywhere was many years later, following graduation from medical school. After buying the first car, I drove with my wife Sally and our six-month-old daughter Susan from Syracuse, New York to Boston, Massachusetts for the start of my medical internship.

The northern border of Central Park is 110th Street and the western park entrance on Eighth Avenue was within easy walking distance from the apartment house. Pop would take me there on Sundays to sail my handsome boat in the Conservatory pond, and, in springtime, we would return home with a bouquet of Mom's favorite flower, lilacs.

And in the spring and summer, Mom and I used to take a prepared lunch for Pop down to Madison Square Park, way downtown at 23rd Street. This was either via the El or on a spectacular journey in an open-air, double-decker bus down residential Fifth Avenue at the eastern border of Central Park. The apartment houses were huge and had interestingly worked masonry facades. When we passed the impressive Metropolitan Museum of Art, I knew that the graceful, white fountain at 59th Street was not far off. It was the place where expensive looking carriages, pulled by horses and driven by colorfully dressed coachmen in top hats, were gathered, waiting for passengers who wanted to see the sights of Central Park. And below 59th Street, Fifth Avenue became a fashionable business street with tall office buildings, shops and an occasional church, like St. Patrick's.

Morningside Avenue had horse and wagon delivery for milk and ice, but I had been born too late to see the awesome, horse-driven fire engines clanging their way on the pavement. However, Mom's vivid descriptions, especially of the hook and ladder and the smoke and spark-belching steamer truck, were good substitutes.

North of 110th Street was Harlem's major cross town, commercial thoroughfare, 125th Street. The Regent Theatre there was the place for seeing movies, and my cousin Fortuna used to take me every Saturday afternoon. A vanilla malted milk and a soft pretzel at the candy store before the movie was routine, as was a paper bag of penny candy to carry into the theatre. One of the first movies I saw, as I was becoming a movie buff, was the Phantom of the Opera, starring Lon Chany,

Sr. I have never forgotten the scary face and the episode where he was swimming under water in the sewers while breathing from a tube projecting above the surface. Perhaps for that reason, I was never later attracted to snorkeling.

East of Harlem, on the other side of Manhattan, was Park Avenue, which at 125th Street was not a classy residential area as it is near Grand Central Station, but a place where itinerant merchants, for the most part Jewish, sold goods and produce from push carts. Occasionally I would accompany my Uncle Ezra, an immigrant from Baghdad in Iraq, when he went shopping there. He was a silver-handlebar mustached patriarch who had become an oriental rug merchant on Fifth Avenue. He loved to bargain for and bring home the choicest fruits and vegetables.

Seeing him at the Yom Kippur service in the Spanish-Jewish synagogue strengthened my conception of him as a patriarch. During a particularly hushed and reverent reading of the text, he was the congregation member who stood at the closed doors of the Ark. Strangely, instead of a yarmulke, he was wearing his gray felt fedora hat. His prayer shawl, draped from the top of his fedora, hung in front of his face, as he murmured the holy words. I never really understood the context, but I surmised it was some important communication with the On High.

My world at 246 Manhattan Avenue extended up one flight of stairs from our top floor. This was the roof where the laundry was hung to dry in the sun. Nona and Mom would have done the laundry in the kitchen sink, using a washboard, wrung it out by hand, after which it and I were carried up to the fresh air of the roof. And the roof had other uses also. It was a fine place to observe the full solar eclipse, looking at the sun through many layers of dark, exposed photographic negatives. But what I remember about it is the eerie, slow-paced darkening of the daylight and the quietness, which descended during the experiencing of the awesome phenomenon.

Much later, when I was teaching graduate students about the necessity of control observations in experimental research, I referred them to a book, which described a cohort of frightened tribesmen, panicked at the disappearance of the sun during a complete solar eclipse. By beating drums they hoped to get the sun to return. The maneuver never failed them since it always came back!

My family left Harlem in late 1927 and so my world moved to the Bronx. But that is another story.

Summer 1928

On the *Ile de France*

For years Mathilde had yearned to return to Turkey and see her parents once again. Somehow it never happened. In November 1925, Mathilde gave birth, at home as was the custom then, to a second son, David. This event was a huge surprise to their 4-year-old son Joseph, who had no idea that he was about to become a brother. His cousin, Fortuna, offered to take Joseph out for the day. They went to the movies and saw "The Hunchback of Notre Dame" and then had lunch together. When they arrived home and Joseph found his mother Mathilde in bed with a tiny baby boy, Joseph was enchanted and thoroughly confused.

Then in 1927 Mathilde received the news that her mother, Joya, had died. Great was Mathilde's sadness and sorrow. The only thing that could make her smile was time spent with their baby son, David, now two years old, but even that didn't always work. Her husband, Mark, finally decided that a trip abroad would lift her spirits, and he could make it into a business trip also.

And so, in the early summer of 1928, Mark and Mathilde and their sons, Joseph and David, boarded the *Isle de France* in New York city, and the adventure began. Several people came along. Accompanying them were Mathilde's sister, Cadem, and her husband, Ezra; their three children, Fortuna, Morris, and Rae; plus Mazal and Nissim Emmanuel, friends of Mathilde and Mark, and their three daughters.

Once aboard ship, Joseph was fascinated, and swiftly began to explore every nook and cranny. He went running all over the ship, checking out the playroom, the athletic room, the dining salon, and the library, which held his attention for a long time. He was intrigued by the writing desks complete with pens for passengers who wished to write letters or cards. They looked as if they were made of carved ivory. And one pen had a lens at one end, and when you looked through it, you saw a picture of a nude woman!

Mark (or "Pop" as his children called him) was in paradise. He liked walking the deck with Mathilde. And he enjoyed playing shuffleboard and quoits with Joseph. What a wonderful experience for this man who had worked so hard all his life!

Meals were greatly enjoyed, as they all gathered together in the dining salon. Mathilde, although impressed with the food presentation, was never quite convinced that the cooking was as good as hers.

The days passed so swiftly, as the ship sailed eastward towards France. Suddenly the ship was approaching LeHavre, France. Such excitement. Where were the children? Did they have all their baggage? Almost before they knew what was happening they were off the ship and aboard a train headed for Paris.

Paris!

You can imagine the excitement as they arrived in Paris and settled into a hotel there. Of course, with so many people traveling together, getting anything accomplished was a major event. They would start out somewhere, but, inevitably, someone would have forgotten something or someone would have to go to the bathroom, and everyone would have to wait. Things moved very slowly.

But they had such wonderful times. Joseph recalls rolling a hoop in the park, Punch and Judy Shows on the Champs Elysées, visiting the Tomb of an Unknown Soldier at the Arc de Triomphe, Versailles with its Hall of Mirrors and great gardens. Once they ate fresh almonds at a restaurant. Mark made certain that Joseph saw the important sites. He took them on a bus tour of the battlefields of World War One and later, another bus tour to Reims to see the great cathedral.

The men of course had their important work to do. As shopkeepers in New York City, they spent a good part of their time in Paris ordering merchandise. Mark, who was in business with his brother Alex, sold trunks and suitcases and ladies handbags; Ezra, Cadem's husband, sold oriental rugs. Both men felt very comfortable in Paris, since they could speak French well, thanks to their having studied at *Alliance Française* in Turkey. The days flew by, and then one evening Mark, Ezra, and Nissim agreed that they had accomplished their business tasks, had made the necessary arrangements or purchases, and they were ready to take off for Egypt at any time.

"*A dio!*" groaned the women, as if this announcement came as a complete surprise. And, to be sure, packing everything up and moving on again would probably be almost as difficult as setting forth from New York. However, they all agreed that they were eager to move on. And so the packing began, along with the reluctant "last visits" to all their favorite spots in that magnificent city.

Paris to Marseille

The Paris railway station was filled with moving people, surging this way and that, brushing occasionally against little David and his parents, who were awaiting the arrival of the train for Marseille. His seven-year-old brother, Joseph, sat quietly, reading. His father, Mark, consulted his watch with an air of importance befitting a man of business visiting France; his mother, Mathilde, stared anxiously in the direction from which the train should come, looking as if she would make a jump for it as soon as she heard its approach for fear of missing it; and little David, all in white—shorts, shirts, socks and shoes—hair wetly combed, watched the people passing. Suddenly he began to fidget and pulled Mathilde's hand, until she bent down so that he might whisper loudly into her ear.

"Mama, I have to go."

Mathilde nodded to Mark and led David off to the room marked *"Femmes,"* but as they reached the doorway David shook his hand free, saying firmly, "Not here. This is for ladies."

Mathilde tried to reason, telling him that it made no difference, that they would miss the train, but David just shook his sleek head.

"Well, then, I will get Papa to take you." And they turned around and returned to Mark, to whom Mathilde explained what had happened.

Mark beamed and, turning to David, said, "So now you are a man, eh?"

But David just squirmed until Mark proudly took him toward the doorway marked *"Hommes,"* leaving Mathilde standing beside the suitcases. Once inside, David impatiently dispensed with his father's offers of assistance and efficiently took care of the situation himself. As he and Mark left the room they could hear the train puffing its way into the station, and they could see Mathilde, frantically beckoning them to hurry. David looked up at Mark, who grinned, then they both purposely sauntered slowly and nonchalantly over to Mathilde, who was all but jumping up and down for fear they would miss the train. Joseph went on reading.

"Be easy, Mathilde," laughed Mark. "My son and I have returned from our little errand now, so you needn't worry. Besides the train won't be leaving for some time yet."

But Mathilde gently closed Joseph's book, picked up the smallest suitcase and, indicating that Mark should pick up the two remaining bags, she coaxed all three of them toward the train, acting like a mother hen with two errant chicks. They boarded their car and seated themselves, then waited for the train to move, Mark looking importantly at the golden watch, just to let others know that this trip was not purely a pleasure trip, that he was a man of affairs with business to transact. Joseph returned to his book. David sat docilely between his parents watching all the compartments fill up, until finally the train lurched forward, and David was placed next to the window so that he might see the countryside.

With nose pressed to the glass, he looked out over the fields, the towns, the vineyards of France until he grew tired and leaned against his mother to sleep, and the train whirled on through the countryside, whistling out at the approaching villages. Inside, there was only the sound of an occasional snoring sleeper or the turn of a newspaper page.

David woke and went back to the window and the advancing-receding panorama once more, his still sleepy eyes dazzled by the sunlight. He turned to his parents.

"I'm thirsty."

Laying down his newspapers, Mark stood up, took from the rack overhead a glass and a full bottle of Vichy water, which he uncorked. He then filled the glass and handed it to his little son, who sipped, gagged and spat it out, thrusting the glass back at his father.

"I want water," he said loudly. "That's not water."

Mark tried to press the glass back into David's unwilling hand, telling him the water on the train was unclean and that Vichy water was what he must drink; but the child clenched his fists, placed them behind his back, and turning his head away began to howl.

"I want water!"

A flurry of commotion took place. Sleepers closed their mouths and awoke, diners looked up from their crusty bread and cheese, and readers put down their books. All looked to see what was causing the child to cry; what was being done to the child to have him make such a noise?

"*Voici,*" said a man to Mark. "This will quench the thirst of the little one," and the man handed him a bottle of wine, but Mark, who was annoyed with his child, passed the bottle to Mathilde saying,

"See if this is what your child wants."

And he hid behind his newspaper, leaving Mathilde to look doubtfully at the bottle of red wine, then shrug her shoulders and say softly to her little one, "Here, my darling. This will take away your thirst."

David stopped howling, and with head still averted, asked,

"Is that water?"

"Better than water," crooned Mathilde.

"I don't want it," he sobbed. "I WANT WATER."

Mathilde looked helplessly at her husband, and she heard someone mutter, "The child must be dreadfully spoiled."

At this Mark rattled his newspaper, but continued reading, while the distressed passengers began to gather about him and Mathilde and child. They offered many suggestions, none of which impressed the red-faced, tear-stained David, who was no longer crisp in his white attire but wrinkled and sweating.

He howled and cried and kept on crying, until at last there came a lull in all the noises, the people having run out of ideas, and having stopped for breath. Then came a voice not yet heard from.

"If he wants water—give him water."

On hearing these words even David himself was compelled along with the others to turn and stare and see huddled in the corner a very old, shriveled and shrunken woman, all in black. Everyone began gesticulating and explaining to her, while David again commenced to sob, that the child should not have the water because it had not been purified and it was not fit to drink; but since the child had come from America, where everything is clean, he did not understand this. Then they turned back to the howling child, and again came the voice.

"Give him the water. Can a simple thing like water do more harm than the crying?"

The people were silent, then one by one they began to nod, and finally one went away with a glass and returned it brimming full with water. The train lurched just then and the water sloshed about, wetting David on his bare knee, so that he cautiously looked about and seeing the glass asked, "Is it water?"

When his mother nodded, he took the glass in both hands and drank it greedily. Then, glass empty, he looked with annoyance at the circle of people about him, with a what-are-you-staring-at look, and turned away from them toward the window until the people dispersed, returning to their books and their naps.

Afterwards when he could see from the reflection in his

window that they had all gone, he turned and looked at the old woman in the corner, and she smiled a triumphant, toothless, gummy smile, and he blinked at her, then returned to the window to look out upon the world as the train rushed southward.

On to Egypt

In Marseille they boarded the ship, *Champolion,* by now of course they considered themselves experienced travelers and were more relaxed and easy as they headed towards Alexandria, Egypt. They worried not about water for the young David. They smiled at one another and enjoyed the voyage.

In the middle of the night their ship passed the volcano Stromboli, which was shooting magnificent sparks, and Mathilde woke her son, Joseph, and took him up to the deck just to make sure he saw it.

As they approached Alexandria, Mathilde began to brood, wondering if she would even recognize any of her family, or they, her. She'd been in America for fifteen years! There had been so many changes in all that time. For one thing, her sister Esther was now married, with children; and their father, Papa David, had left Turkey after his wife's death and was now living in Egypt with Esther. She leaned on the ship's railing, brooding; and little David, always sensitive to his mother's moods, began to hover about her and try to lift her spirits.

Then, suddenly, they were very close to shore, and Mathilde could see all the people standing on shore. There! There was her sister, Esther, and those children surrounding her must be hers! Esther was waving enthusiastically. Mathilde began to smile, and then started to assemble her own family so that they might get off the boat and get close to her family as soon as she could.

They stayed with Aunt Esther and her husband and their children, Odette, Eli, and David. Their large apartment was across the street from the King's Palace. From the windows at Aunt Esther's they could see the Pyramids.

There was a great reunion with all the relatives who lived there. For Mathilde it was like a dream come true, and as the days passed and she mixed and mingled with her sisters and their families and their father, she felt quite joyous. Yes, her mother, Joya, was gone. But oh, the pleasures to be had in cooking together and shopping and taking care of the children! The laughter and chatter and singing! It was almost like old times when they all gathered together in the big kitchen in Turkey.

Both Joseph and David finally got to meet their grandfather David Abraham. Almost as soon as they entered the apartment, Joseph went over to Papa David and kissed him. Joseph was able to recognize his grandfather because he'd seen a photograph of him at home.

The boys were impressed with Ezra, who seemed very different in Egypt. Decades later they still recalled that he had a horsehair wand for getting at flies, which were numerous there. And they also remembered that he used to say "Yalah!" in a very loud voice, to ward off aggressive merchants.

The days melted away, and they continued to enjoy all being together. Then, suddenly, it was late August and time to return to New York and work and school. The wonderful holiday was almost over. Of course, they all promised to do this sort of thing again in the future. Soon! Soon! And then they did their packing and made preparations to leave Egypt.

They returned at last to America, traveling once again on the *Ile de France*. One day Mark discovered to his great surprise that an airplane on a catapult was on board, covered by a large tarp. When the ship was two days out of New York City, the French sailors began removed canvas coverings etc. And, one day before docking in New York, the airplane, which was carrying mail from Europe, was launched – and the mail reached New York a day ahead of schedule.

So, back to New York City and the Bronx and the routine of long, hard days of work for Pop, school for Joseph, and the domestic routine for Mathilde. Mark's mother, Rebecca, or "Nona" as they called her, was delighted to welcome them back.

They, none of them, ever forgot their wonderful fairytale journey across the Atlantic to France, the train trips, the boat to Egypt, Egypt itself, and all their loving relatives there, and finally the journey back home to New York City and seeing the Statue of Liberty once again. They never made another trip like that, but for Joseph in particular the trip must have been enormously influential. His eyes were wide open.

Ke Bendicho Padre

"Such an adorable child!" Mathilde will often say. "So beautiful!" And her eyes sparkle and you sense her pleasure. Always, Mathilde has attended to the beauty of small children, and she has been most generously vocal in sharing her appreciation with others.

An adolescent when she came to America in the early years of the twentieth century, Mathilde lived for an enchanted period of time with a wealthy manufacturer of Turkish cigarettes and his family in Larchmont. Pampered and adored by them, she led a fairy tale existence. She learned English, played tennis on their very own courts, and basked in the knowledge that she was considered special. As the youngest of ten children growing up in Turkey, being a single jewel rather than one of a cluster was an experience to be treasured.

In the early 1920s she married and settled into a more prosaic life in the Bronx, caring for husband, apartment and two sons. For her, the happiest period in her adult life remains still that time when her boys were young. "So gorgeous, with skin like ripe peaches." Tossing all thoughts of matronly dignity to the wind, she used to fall to her knees before these little kings and play and sing the afternoons away.

Still her life was a busy one. In the Bronx—or for that matter, wherever Sephardic women draw breath—daily life for a housewife is well scheduled. Always a little housework in the morning followed by preparations for dinner, the custom being to do the serious cooking well in advance—the meats, the chickens, the vegetables bathed in tomato sauces and oils—then preheated for the evening meal. Like so much of Mediterranean cooking, these meals are taste delights, drawing liberally upon fresh vegetables, cheeses, sauces and the like.

Following lunch, which consists often of tidbits hoarded from the previous evening's meal, Mathilde, like other Sephardic wives, dresses and prepares to go out. A little shopping, perhaps for fresh rolls from the neighborhood bakery, or the careful selection of some fruit. Then she permits herself to visit with friends, unless friends are coming to visit her. Not for these women the pleasures of a coffee or tea shop. No indeed, entertaining is best done at home—the food is better!

And in this fashion, Mathilde often sets forth on a weekday afternoon, handbag over her arm. She descends the four flights of stairs from their walkup apartment, and eventually, after her afternoon shopping, visits the apartments of friends. This generally involves more stair climbing, as most of her friends prefer to live up a flight or two. The air so much fresher, the views of the Grand Concourse so much more charming. It is summer, and Mathilde is wearing a light print dress, some jewelry, of course, and white shoes to match her summer handbag. Freshly anointed with lilac cologne, her favorite scent, she smells good as always.

One afternoon she rings the bell of a certain household, and a tiny two-year-old boy of great beauty flings the door open. Mathilde's eyes widen in appreciation. She knows beauty in children, for has she not herself two sons of extraordinary beauty indeed? And this child is the grandson of a dear friend with whom she has been acquainted since school days in Turkey.

"Ah, *ke bendicho padre!*" Mathilde exclaims, for truly the Lord has spoken well in this young child.

"Mathilde, what a pleasure," says her friend. "Come in. We must have coffee."

"That child—so adorable," says Mathilde. "I could eat him up."

And so the little scene is played out, for Mathilde has seen this beautiful child before and will see him again. Turkish coffee, prepared in a *librik* by the hostess, is brought forth foaming, before being poured into tiny cups. Cookies are passed and urged upon the visitor. Always water is served in tall glasses, and sometimes fruit.

"Take, take," the visitor is urged. "So you're having dinner soon, what does it matter? Fruit won't fill anybody up."

And the little child grows taller over the years, eventually coming to call Mathilde "Mrs. Bendichopadre" as a joke.

It's pleasant to spend the late afternoon in this manner, gossiping with old friends, holding a child, for Mathilde's boys are now too big for this indignity. Eventually she collects her parcels and handbag, says goodbye and clatters down the flights of steps. As she walks along the handsome Concourse where dappled shade from the plane trees protects her from the sun's heat, she looks like something of a child herself—short and sturdy frame, topped by a mop of dark curls, with her eyes, large and gray, always looking out at the world with curiosity.

She makes the long climb up to apartment 4A, and then bustles into the kitchen, renewed for the evening preparations, which are fairly simple. The advance work pays off. Here are the vegetables simmering nicely, here the pot roast already sliced and ready to be thrust into the oven, there the obligatory Spanish rice, tinted pale pink from its tomato liquid, fluffy with each grain separate from the others. Mathilde is justly proud of her reputation in the community for making the best rice around. The table is set by the window to catch any breeze passing by. Now she has only to put out the Calamata olives, make a little salad. It is seven o'clock. Soon her husband will be climbing the stairs and everything will be in readiness.

Years roll by, and somewhere in the middle of the century a terrible war comes. Many of the most beautiful and beloved of children are hurled into the brunt of it and killed, maimed, wounded. There is much pain and sorrow. Mathilde's older son Joseph becomes a soldier and is severely wounded on a tiny island half a world away. Her cries of anguish "*A dio, a dio,*" echo up and down the Concourse, and nothing her husband or her younger son say can ease her pain.

"He is not dead," her husband says; and "It's only his leg wounded," David, the younger son adds. Mathilde stares at them without speaking.

Only the visits from friends and other women in the neighborhood, who moan and cry with her, help to lessen her anguish. "Your beautiful first-born," one starts, and another carries on, "Wounded, oh it's terrible, terrible," and they all cry, Mathilde along with them, and somehow in this way she is faintly consoled. From his bedroom, the younger brother listens and concludes that as soon as he turns eighteen he must do the right thing. On the day after his birthday he joins the navy.

The war is over, and Mathilde's boys are returned home safely, thanks to God. Mathilde has agreed to meet her husband Mark after he finishes work, so that they may celebrate their wedding anniversary. They are standing in a long line at Radio City Music Hall, having been lured there along with thousands of other theatergoers by the promise of a personal stage appearance by Tallulah Bankhead. Mathilde is wearing her navy silk dress with a print top. Over her arm she has a navy leather bag, which goes nicely with her matching sling pumps. She carries also a shopping parcel from Macy's. Her back aches. Mark, who is tall and thin, wears a gray suit and gray fedora. He has a rolled newspaper under his arm.

Slowly they shuffle forward in the line that winds almost completely around the block. They stand, shifting their weight from one foot to the other. "At least it's not raining," says Mark, and Mathilde nods.

They stand there for an incredibly long time. Can the movie; can Tallulah herself possibly be worth it? Mathilde asks herself.

At long last they reach the doorway, shuffle, shuffle, then finally they are within the magnificent building itself, although still the double line snakes around within the great lobby. Mathilde's eyes sparkle, and she nudges Mark with her elbow. She never tires of the robust beauty of Radio City Music Hall. No matter how often she comes here, she still basks in the splendor of the glittering chandeliers, the acres of crimson carpeting, which extend even up the broad circular stairway. What beauty! Perhaps for her this is a partial fulfillment of the quest that brought her to America. Mark also seems never to tire of coming to this theatre, usually considered a place for tourists. Already he is looking forward to hearing yet again the magnificent organ and seeing the Rockettes dance with such precision. Mark and Mathilde are happy.

Just then, at that very moment, as they are looking about the vast lobby with satisfied awe, for after all they are a part of this incredible city, this unbelievably splendid country—at that very moment, a tall uniformed young man wearing a cape lined with crimson swoops down upon Mathilde; and before the eyes of the waiting thousands, this dashing figure sweeps Mathilde, along with her escort Mark, up to the very head of the long winding line! Surely, with the length of the line, they would have had to wait another forty-five minutes before reaching this spot. Did someone guess it was their anniversary? Mathilde knows that everyone is looking at them. Well! Tallulah will have to put on a really good act to match this one!

Then Mathilde, small of frame and possessing still those luminous eyes of childhood, looks up to see who has transported her to the head of the line. She is, at first, puzzled; who can this handsome young man be? His back is to them as he prepares to open the doors that will permit Mathilde and Mark to be the first people to enter the great auditorium. Then he turns swiftly, the cape swirling, and leans down to speak into her ear.

"Mrs. Bendichopadre, it will always be a pleasure to open doors for you!"

Nona
by
Joseph M. Benforado

No one could have had a grandmother like my Nona. When I think of her, my father's mother, I remember that I'm a first generation American. I think about her often because, with love and affection, she shaped the way I, her first grandson, grew up.

Nona was a widow whose husband, after whom I was named, had died unexpectedly while the family was living in Smyrna, Turkey. The year was 1898, and the eldest of three children was only eight years old. Although unable to read or write, Nona was undaunted. She opened a laundry and sewing business to maintain the family. A strong-willed person, she was to become the family matriarch.

Nona and the three sons immigrated to the United States just after 1910. The young men gained new citizenship but she remained an alien who never learned to speak English. Her language was Ladino, often called Judeo-Spanish. The Sephardim, who were descendants of Jews expelled from Spain in 1492, the year that Columbus discovered America, spoke this Old Spanish.

When I was born in New York City in 1921, I already had a built-in grandmother because Nona had lived with my parents from the day they were married. Ladino, also my mother's family tongue, was therefore my first language. English, which my parents learned in night school, came later. My use of Ladino reflected Nona's use. I could speak it but I never read or wrote it. My wife now uses the term "Kitchen Spanish" for the way Nona and I communicated with each other.

Nona devoted much of her day to working in the kitchen. Every morning on school days she prepared sandwiches carefully, using a rubber band to secure the wax paper coverings. Nona expected me to return the bands to the kitchen drawer when I came home. Often as not I forgot or just plain lost them. She was, however, patient with me and, in an unruffled way, she would ask my father to bring more rubber bands home from his office.

Meals were always an important part of her day's activity. In later years when my wife and I made trips with our children to visit my family, Nona would often remark to my mother at dinner, in Ladino of course, " The little ones are not eating anything". But she also adapted to new ways. She served milk to the children with all meals, even when meat was the main dish. This deviation from Jewish tradition arose because the family physician had recommended it for the health of growing children!

The beneficence of food was the basis for a remark, now a family classic, which Nona once made as we were leaving the table following an ample, deliciously prepared, Sephardic supper. I must have been eleven or twelve. She had handed me an apple and I said, "Nona, I'm not hungry." Her reply was "You don't have to be hungry to eat an apple!"

Nona, Rebecca Sides, was born in Greece and I often enjoyed looking up in the school atlas, the various cities she had lived in. The exotic sounding names still trip off my tongue: Volos, Larissa, and Trikala. Some years ago, when attending a museum talk on Greece, I was reminded of Nona for a strange reason. There was a slide showing an island monastery high above a cliffside, with pulleys being used as elevators for food supplies for human beings as well. Strangely enough, Nona made use of a somewhat related principle when I was a kid. We were living on the fourth floor of an apartment house without an elevator, and the kitchen window opened on a courtyard where I played with my friends. When it was time for afternoon crackers or a piece of fruit, Nona would send the food down in a small basket suspended by a heavy cord.

Nona had Sephardic women friends, of her generation, who, like her, had come to the states with family. Also like her, they had never learned English. Among them were *Tia* Miriam, *Ermana* Sarina, and *Madame* Galindos. The reasons for the varying titles were never clear to me.

The friends lived in our neighborhood and visited each other often. When it was Nona's turn to host a get-together or to have the sewing circle, I took care of the refreshments whenever I was at home. I would serve the sweet followed by demitasses of Turkish coffee. As I was growing up, I had learned to help Nona at the appropriate season with the making of the sweets: *Vi°na*, a preparation of boiled cherries in thick sugar syrup; *chitra* a candied grapefruit rind also in a syrup; and *brimbrio*, a dried quince jam. Nona taught me to pit cherries, using one of her formidable, sturdy hairpins, how to scrape the pulp from grapefruit rind, and how to wrap towels around her forearms before she started stirring the huge pots on the stove. And by the time I was twelve, I was using the long-handled brass *librik* or coffee pot for making the Turkish coffee. I was particularly skilled in partitioning the *kaimok*, or froth, evenly among the cups. Brass *libriks*, exactly like the one Nona had, are sold in local coffee houses in Madison. Some things don't change!

Many years ago I chanced to find Irving Stone's "The Greek Treasure" in a used bookshop. It is a biographical novel based on the life of Heinrich Schleimann, the discoverer of the ancient city of Troy in Asia Minor. The site of the excavations was in Turkey, north of Smyrna where both of my parents were born. Of course I bought the book. An early part of the story describes Schleimann visiting a family in Athens, Greece, on an afternoon and being served sweets and Turkish coffee. I could have written the text by describing what I did for Nona's guests. Everything was exactly the same!

The use of a tray containing filled glasses of water, a bowl of *visna*, and a collection of dessert spoons, followed later by demitasses of Turkish coffee. Of particular interest to me was the graceful manner in which the guest chose a spoon, took a bit of the sweet from the bowl, brought it to an open mouth, skillfully without dripping, and followed this with a glass of water. The spoon was then placed back in the same glass. Nona must have learned all this while growing up in Greece. That Schleimann began his excavations a year after Nona was born made it seem all the more like a fairy tale.

Nona's sewing circle was a source of awe to me. The women were sewing shrouds, their own, with material which may have come from Palestine. I do remember Mother telling me that the little head pillows they fashioned, for use in the casket, were filled with earth that had been brought over, for this special use, from the Holy Land. And I later was to learn that Nona and some of her friends were members of an elite group of women in the synagogue congregation. Their task was preparing the bodies of the dead for burial. Edgar Allen Poe had nothing on Nona!

My grandmother valued neatness and cleanliness. She was always well groomed, with gold earrings and with gray hair expertly coiled on the top of her head. An apron over a colorful printed housedress was her usual attire unless she went out visiting. That required a black silk dress and black coat and hat.

Limpio (clean) instead of *suzio* (dirty) was a guiding principle in her life. She and I disagreed from time to time about this, but of course she always won out. Once, before breakfast, I had changed from a freshly laundered striped shirt to a white one. It was a Friday and boys had to wear white shirts for grade school assembly. Nona saw me folding the striped shirt to replace it in the dresser drawer. She took it out of my hands and put it into the laundry hamper. When I protested with "*Ez limpio*' she corrected me. "*Ez suzio.*" She later washed and ironed it to make it *limpio* again.

Cultural mixing has made the United States a melting pot. But can you imagine the stew my wife and I were in when we wanted to get married against the wishes of our respective families, Catholic and Jewish? On my side, it was Nona who bolstered us by providing loving counsel. She said, in Ladino of course, "If you love Sally, and if Sally loves you, and if you are both good people, get married."

And we did, in court.

Epilogue

Table Talk

Forcing my face into a mask of intelligent interest, I abandon any attempt to follow the dinner table conversation, which is switching randomly from French to Spanish to English. I turn my head from one to another of the speakers, though in truth even when I struggle to comprehend, I can grasp only a tenth of what is being said.

We are in Paris, my husband and I, spending an evening in the suburbs with his cousin Odette and her family. As befits a matriarch, she is enthroned at the head of the table, my husband on her right, her husband, Sam, on her left, with myself seated next to him. Their three sons, Claude, André, and Raoul, are down at the lower end of the table interspersed with the beautiful young wives of André and Raoul. Claude, the middle son, who is divorced, is the only one of the three who remembers us from a previous visit, when he was a teenager. "Yes, yes, I remember you," he had said when we arrived, looking at me with intense, melancholy eyes.

Raoul, the eldest son, is seated by my side and, easily handling English, he pours various wines into my glass from time to time as well as keeping up a running commentary of his work and his family life. At the same time he is conducting a humorous drawn-out conversation with his brothers and their wives. *"Comme vous êtes en bonne mine,"* he exclaims to André's wife, and to me, "Charming blouse she is wearing, isn't it?" and to Claude, "How was your party last night? *Amusante?"* He turns to me and I leap in.

"It's so exciting," I say, "to be here, to think that your—and our—children share a great grandfather. Papa David must have been a wonderful man, so kind, so good." I babble on, then pause to drain my glass.

He gives me a thoughtful look.

"Try this wine," he suggests, tipping a ruby-colored liquid in my direction. "I think you will find it has a certain . . . clarity."

Like her son Raoul, Odette has an air of belonging to the world. Languages come easily to her. Since she is the one who picked us up at our hotel in her tidy little Renault and brought us out here, we know that she handles a car with ease as well. True, she's gotten heavier over the years as the family has prospered. But her voice still has that sweet clearness and her warmth shines through. "But no," she had insisted when we told her over the phone of our plans to take the Metro to their house in the suburbs. "I myself will come for you."

When we arrived with Odette at their apartment, Sam greeted us at the door with a hug for each of us. Guiding us through the maze of chairs, little tables, and elaborate floor lamps that ranged about the rooms, he found us comfortable chairs, pressed a light drink into our hands, and smiled kindly at us. He spoke little and sighed from time to time, but whenever his wife ignored a remark someone else had made and plunged into a conversation of her own, he would patiently say, "Odette, you're not letting them finish their story."

Now we are at the dinner table, and one elaborate, unfamiliar course follows another in dizzying succession. I am forced to abandon my musings as the sullen Portuguese maid appears at my side holding a huge platter below my nose. Me first again? How unfair! I don't even know what is being offered me, although it smells and looks delicious. How much to take? How to serve it to myself? Help!

But if the food is unfamiliar to me, perhaps the people with whom I dine are even more puzzling. Descendants of folk born over the centuries, flung outward from Spain to the late fifteenth century, Sephardic Jews who chose to leave their homes and their country, rather than convert to Catholicism at the time of the religious inquisitions. My husband's ancestors settled in Turkey, where they continued to speak over the centuries their native Spanish, as he is doing now. He is likewise a true "international." Mellowed by the wine and the food, he is preparing to tell a joke. Working in Spanish first, switching to French with aplomb, he tells a story of a Turkish beggar who has been summoned before the judge for the heinous crime of smelling shishkebab when he has no money to pay. The irate shishkebab vendor is pleased when the judge declares the beggar guilty and fines him 30 *dinars.* "But judge, *por favor,* I have no money, I cannot pay," gasps the beggar. "Not to worry," announces the judge regally. "*En fin,* I shall pay the fine." He lays the coins on the palm of his hand, and when the greedy vendor stretches forth his hand, the judge shakes his head, rattles the coins beneath the vendor's nose, and says, "But no, you are permitted only to *smell* the money!"

The joke, told well by my husband, creates a sensation at the table and much multilingual conversation follows concerning the morals of the situation, recipes for shishkebab and the like, accompanied by guffaws and applause.

At this point the Portuguese maid is on the scene again, shuffling from chair to chair, removing the dishes in preparation for the next course. She is apparently doing it all wrong somehow. Both Sam and Odette speak loudly to her in an unrecognizable tongue and she answers back heatedly before retreating to the kitchen. Is it Portuguese, I wonder? Good heavens, how many languages do these people speak? It occurs to me at this point that the Portuguese servant is as out of it as I am, poor thing.

At gatherings such as this I regret my ancestors, who came to America so long ago, emigrating from English-speaking countries. Languages have never come easily to me, and while I like my sedate English and Irish ancestry, I envy my husband his ease with language. He grew up, after all, in a trilingual home where French could be utilized if adults wished to talk without the children understanding. How can such people ever know the frustrations of being monolingual?

I turn to Sam, Odette's husband, who is speaking to me in English. He is a kind man with a gentle face, and he is asking me about my family in America. On other occasions when we have been with Sam, he has been exuberant and jolly, but for the past years he has been in a depressed state and his sons and wife are worried. He is trying to entertain me, but it is clearly an effort.

Except for the addition of a moustache, Sam appears much as he did when we first visited them in the late 1950s. He'd taken us to lunch at a restaurant on the Champs Elysées. "I must introduce you to the Parisian two-hour lunch," he had said falling between my husband and me, and linking arms with both of us. They'd been living in Paris only a short time, having been expelled from Egypt along with other Jews and French-speaking people by Nasser's government following the Suez business. Most of their possessions had been left behind and at that time they were just beginning to get back on their feet again.

We saw one another again a decade later when Sam and Odette came to America, and they visited us in western New York State where we were living. Wanting to reciprocate their Parisian hospitality, we had struggled to entertain them at plush restaurants and trips to Niagara Falls, but Odette had said softly after a few days, "We merely wish to be family with you." They brought elaborate toys for our children, good toys like sets of blocks and imaginative little buildings that could be formed into cities.

Sam excuses himself from the table, and his sons follow his departure with their eyes.

Odette leans toward me, touching my sleeve, and occupies me in conversation.

"The children? How are they all?"

I talk with her and confess that I find French difficult. I confide that I studied and reviewed my high school French for many months before making this trip, but that my husband, who did not review at all, still handles the language with much more dexterity. Then we talk about the family, hers and my husband's, and I tell her about the stories I have been writing over the years; stories about their lives in Turkey and about their adventures when some of them immigrated to America in the early 1900s.

At this point my husband decides to tell a story about an experience we'd had at a restaurant in Provence a few days previously. We'd been dining with our daughter there, lingering over coffee, and suddenly a waiter dropped some cups, which fell to the floor with a loud crash. Without even thinking, my husband instinctively said *"capará!"* a word his mother and grandmother and aunts and cousins have always said whenever anything got broken. A sort of warding off of evil spirits. Immediately the conversation at the adjoining table in the restaurant ceased, and the young woman seated there, who appeared to be Arabic, stared at us thoughtfully.

An interminable conversation erupts here at Odette's table. From Spanish to French to Spanish again. Is *capará* a superstition or a religious belief? What does it mean? Who can translate? Raoul's wife, who is Russian, proceeds to discuss various superstitions of that culture. André and Claude argue about whether the young women in the restaurant had understood the meaning of the word or not. And so on.

We are eating a chocolate torte now, rich and dark, served not by the Portuguese maid but cut into generous wedges by Odette herself, who had made it. The servant stands back against the wall watching. Am I mistaken or is she rolling her eyes at the extended conversation?

What is the point? Why must they go on like this? And my husband, the American from the Bronx . . . when had he turned into this suave cosmopolitan man?

I have a brief conversation with the little wife of André. How many children? she asks. And we talk. How many, how old, etc. Charming little phrases flutter between us—*bon, bien, pas mal*—but it's very limiting to be conversing in fractured French along with hand gestures. The beauty of the young wives, one dark and one blonde, and their way of dressing awes me. The three brothers run a clothing business, which wholesales to England, Italy, and Spain. Yet I can't help feeling the women are somewhat provincial, they're so limited in their handling of languages.

Good heavens, are André and Claude still talking about the philosophical manifestations of *capará,* and whether it's religion or superstition and does it do any good? I have some ideas on the subject, but how to insert them into this linguistic mélange? Odette reaches over and lays a plump ringed hand on mine. "I have a story for you," she says softly. "My mother," she begins in her clear voice, "married a Frenchman who was living in Egypt and they settled in Alexandria where I was born and grew up."

"Oh yes," I say with interest, absently helping myself to the cheese being passed around.

"When my grandmother, Joya, died in Smyrna, grandfather became very lonely and he came to live with us in Alexandria."

"Ah," I say, and I tell Odette that Papa David is one of my favorite characters. I'd written stories about that grandfather, the father of such a large family who so loved his children.

Odette cocks an eyebrow. "He was a tyrant," she says flatly. "Always had to be the boss. Well, when he came to live in our house, he found my father was the boss. We spoke French in our home, and it made my grandfather unhappy because Spanish was his language. He wanted us to speak Spanish at the table, but we seemed always to lapse into French, because it was more comfortable." She pauses. "Try that little white cheese there," she commands, and I do. Delicious.

My world is rocking. Here I sit, eating white cheese while my version of the world, Grandpa David, crumbles all to bits.

Odette continues. "One night my grandfather became very angry at his inability to comprehend the sounds around the table and at his powerlessness to force his people to speak in a language he could understand. He became so angry that he picked up his end of the table and tipped over the whole thing." And she laughs, remembering.

"But . . . he was such a gentle man," I insist, having forgotten that I never really even met this man, had only heard of him through others, mainly through my mother-in-law, that superb teller of tales.

"He was a tyrant," she repeats flatly. "Well, he never came to the table again. *My* father, a very gentle man, told him that if he could not behave himself he should eat alone, and to the end of his life he did." She sighs, then says, "My father was different, he didn't like to be the tyrant. Grandpa David had a ring on his hand and every day he used to make all the children and people come and kiss his ring. An old custom. My father refused to carry it on. He hated the custom." She breaks off here, summoning the maid to her. "Take away the cheeses," she commands. "Bring in the fruits."

I think briefly of overturning the table myself, cutlery, goblets, platters of fruit all cascading to the floor, bringing all talk to a halt.

But no, I take a golden pear instead.

Printed in the United States
43761LVS00002B/211